DIRTY WIFE GAMES

CLARISSA WILD

MUSIC PLAYLIST

"Logos" by Ludovico Einaudi
"Violent Delights Have Violent Ends" by Ramin Djawadi
"Hungry Like The Wolf" by Snow Hill
"Technically, Missing" by Trent Reznor & Atticus Ross
"What Have We Done To Each Other" by Trent Reznor & Atticus Ross
"A Reflection" by Trent Reznor & Atticus Ross
"Daydream" by Ruelle
"Game of Survival" by Ruelle
"Obsession" by Golden State (Animotion Cover)
"Last Stand" by Kwabs
"Papi Pacify" by FKA Twigs
"Burning Desire" by Lana Del Rey
"I Started A Joke" by ConfidentialMX ft. Becky Hanson
"My Body" by Perfume Genius
"Come Say Hello" by Superhumanoids
"Are We Having A Party" by Cliff Martinez
"Ritual Spirit" by Massive Attack & Azekel

PROLOGUE

Accompanying Song: "What Have We Done To Each Other" by Trent Reznor & Atticus

DRAKE

On a cloudy day, the sun bursts through the sky, blinding me, and it was at that moment of squinting as I held my hand above my eyes that I first laid eyes on her.

A young girl with hair as black as soot, dancing in the park and waving her hands, with a smile so pretty it could stop hearts. Her face one I would remember for the rest of my life.

She was frail and thin, just like I was. We were kids, playing in the park, just like everyone else. But this was no normal encounter. Not to me.

On my little bike, I drove in circles, gawking at her,

always trying to catch her attention, but she never looked my way.

The only thing she could focus on was showing her parents a new trick she'd learned. Jumping rope twice in a row. Playing hopscotch while covering her eyes. A new dance.

Every week, she came here. Sometimes, it was on different days.

And because she was here, so was I.

You see, a boy always knows exactly when he's met the girl he's meant to be with.

She was that girl.

She didn't know I wanted to get to know her.

That I even existed.

But even at such a young age, I knew … deep down in my heart … that she would be mine. One day.

If I could muster the courage to approach her.

Only if.

Because I wasn't a courageous little boy. On the contrary, I was a bumbling, shy, and quiet boy, who always sat in the back of the class, daydreaming of another life. Busy with the stories I was penning down on the pages of my notebook.

I wasn't the kid to walk up to a girl and ask her to play with me.

No, I was the kid who silently watched her from afar … admiring her beauty. Her will. Her devotion toward her parents and her ability to keep the hope alive that they one day might care.

Because her parents never seemed happy.

They never laughed or smiled when she did her special thing.

They never talked to her, other than to tell her no.

They never even acknowledged her, except for when it was time to go.

And honestly, it surprised me they even came to the park that often. I guess keeping up appearances was that important to them.

I should've known that before it was too late.

Before I realized that one day was going to be the last day she'd come to the park; the day she was sent to boarding school. Before I knew I may never see her again.

But I did know one thing ...

I would never give up finding her.

Even if it took me a lifetime.

Part I
The Encounter

1

Accompanying Song: "Violent Delights Have Violent Ends" by Ramin Djawadi

Hyun

From the moment I first saw my stalker, I was captivated.

The man with the black leather jacket and dark, spiky hair sits on a bench across the street from my house, staring down at a notebook.

Every night, he sits there at exactly ten p.m., looking off into the distance or writing his notes under the street light … or looking straight at me.

Like he is now.

Our eyes meet, and a sudden electrical current rushes through my veins.

I'm unable to look away from his piercing blue eyes, and I wonder … How long ago did he first see me?

I've only noticed him outside recently … watching over my house as if he's guarding it. Guarding *me*.

I don't know if I should be scared. If I should run or call the cops.

He's never come close.

So is there any reason to act?

As long as he maintains his distance … an invisible line he doesn't cross … I still feel safe. I can survive, knowing he is there, wherever I go.

I never know when or where I'm going to see him again.

I just know I will.

A hampered breath leaves my throat as he stares me down from across the street. His gaze feels like it penetrates through the closed windows. And for a brief second, I think I spot a hint of a smile.

***

The next morning

I wake to the sound of people talking on the radio. It's my clock, which I've set to nine a.m. Not because I have to work. Not today. No, it's because I like my routine, and the stability it gives me. Time is the only constant in this world, and it follows me wherever I go. The only thing I can control—how much time I spend on certain tasks and when I choose to do something. Time is the only one thing I can trust to be truthful.

I press the button and turn off the radio then push away the blanket and sit up straight. I grab my birth control pill and take one along with some water. I put my socks on, yawning. Stumbling through my room, I grab a pair of jeans and a blouse from my closet and put them on. Then I head to my window, open the curtains, and stare outside. The sun blinds me for a moment, but as my eyes adjust and gaze at the bench across my house, I breathe a sigh of relief.

Empty, just like always.

My heart calms as I go into the kitchen to make myself a cup of coffee and prepare some toast. I eat with the television turned on; the noise of the people talking makes me feel more comfortable. Being home alone isn't the greatest thing in the world … not when you've been living in silence for more than a month.

It's not normal, I know that. Normal people find company. They make friends. They invite people into their home and have dinners and parties.

Not me.

I'm the girl who mistrusts every living person on this planet.

It wasn't always this way, though … but like all people, my past shaped me into the person I am today.

I'd rather be alone, hiding in plain sight. It's the

only way to remain safe.

I finish my breakfast and put my dishes in the sink then grab my keys and wallet and walk out the door.

However, I don't move an inch when I notice what's on my front porch.

A small stone ... and underneath it is a piece of paper just big enough to fit in my hand.

I bend over and reach for it, pushing the rock aside as I wonder if this note was meant for me or for someone else. But then I read the words ... and realize this couldn't be for anyone else.

I saw you watching me.

Goose bumps scatter on my skin. I feel unsettled.

It's not a handwritten note ... it's typed. Someone put effort into giving me this message.

My fingers tremble as I hold the note. I look ahead at the street, left and right, but no one's there. I'm all alone with this note that gives me a pang in my stomach.

As I take a deep breath, I crumple it up in my fist and stuff it into my jacket. Then I go on with my day.

***

A few hours later

With my cart filled with groceries, I make my way to the parking lot of the shopping center. I've been holding off on going outside to get some food for quite some time now, but when the fridge is empty, you have to get something to eat. I had no choice but to go, so now, I have a cart filled to the top with everything I need in the hopes I won't have to return for quite some time.

I quickly push it to my car and unlock it, opening up the back so I can load everything in. But when I look through the windshield of my car, a man standing on the sidewalk across the street stares back at me.

I squeal and drop the bottles of ketchup and mustard, along with the bag of buns and sausages I was holding.

"Do you need help?"

A voice behind me forces me to turn around.

It's a woman in her mid-forties, smiling awkwardly at me. Befuddled, I stare at her for a few seconds before regaining my composure. "No, no, I'm fine."

I quickly go to my knees to pick up the items I dropped.

"You sure?" She tries to reach for my stuff, at

which point I snap.

"Don't," I say, leaning away.

She frowns and takes a step back.

"I ... It's fine. I'm fine. Don't worry about it." I give her a tentative smile, after which she nods a few times and leaves.

When she's gone, I sigh and turn around.

The man is gone. He's no longer on the sidewalk or anywhere else for that matter.

Maybe I never really saw him in the first place.

Maybe I'm losing my mind.

I hastily throw the rest of my purchases into the back of my car and slam the door shut, pushing the cart out of the way. Then I run over to the driver's side to jump in and close my door. I don't even bother to bring the cart back to the store ... or properly put on a seat belt. All I can think about is getting the hell out of here.

But as I put the keys into the ignition and start the car, a voice screams in my mind.

Tells me to stop and look.

Tells me I'm no good.

"What the hell are you doing with the gas pedal?" Greg spits. "I told you to push it, not to ram it with your foot!"

"I'm trying ..." I mutter.

"Not good enough!" He snatches my hand from the steering wheel. "Get your hands off there, you stupid ho."

The names he calls me fly in one ear and go out through the other, just like they always do.

I don't pay much attention to them anymore because I've heard them so many times before. I withstand them because I have no choice or say in the matter. His will is law.

"Get out," he yells, pushing me. "Just get out."

I quickly pull the lever on the door and step out before he smacks me again.

He walks around the car, still berating me. "I knew I should've never let you learn how to drive. Look at what you almost did."

"I didn't—"

"You could've killed us!" He's right in front of me, and whenever he speaks, he spits on my face. "You can't fucking drive!"

"We're in a parking lot …"

"And even there you manage to damage my car!" He pushes me aside and jerks open the door to the driver's seat. But before he sits down, he yells at me again. "Get in the damn car!"

I hasten to the other side and slide into the passenger's seat quietly, trying not to produce too much sound. I don't even dare to say a word. I don't want to give him more reasons to yell. Or worse.

"Can't let a woman do a man's job," he huffs, turning the key in the ignition. "I'll show you how it's done." He looks at me as he puts the gear into reverse and hits the gas. "This is how you drive."

I brush away the sweat drops rolling down the back of my neck, and I take a deep breath, letting it all out. Then I shake my head, put the gear in reverse, and drive out of the parking lot. Like I should've done all along.

2

*Accompanying Song: "Violent Delights Have Violent
Ends" by Ramin Djawadi*

Hyun

A few days later

I've always kept to myself. Not because I'm shy, but because people have always disappointed me. Whether they were my friends, my family … or even my parents—all they did was use me for their own benefit. Give me something good and then take it back again.

No one loved me unconditionally. Not even my parents. So I've come to associate people with lies and manipulation … and maybe I've even started to believe I should take part in this dirty game myself.

One year ago, my parents convinced me to meet with a wealthy bank manager, the son of the CEO, because he'd approached them about his interest in me. I thought it was a joke, but when I met the man, Max Marino, I saw in his eyes that he was speaking the truth. He wanted me to take part in his wicked game.

I should've said no.

But my mind was already agreeing. Why? Because my parents wanted it so badly, and for some reason, I thought if I did this, they'd finally love me.

Silly me.

Of course, the game turned out to be much more than I could handle. Nine girls, all together with three brothers ... and we were vying for their attention. Their love. With sex.

It was sick.

To this day, I still regret ever signing his contract.

Luckily, I got out in time before ...

I sigh, not wanting to reminisce. The memories float back in my head every time I'm at this desk in the library, and I can't help but think about it, but I know I shouldn't. It's not healthy to linger on the past.

Besides, it's time for work, and if my supervisor sees me chilling, I know he'll give me a lecture. One I want to avoid at all cost, considering I got this job through my parents ... and ... Greg.

Just the thought makes me cringe.

I scroll through the list of books as I finish inventory when my eyes catch something peculiar. A man wearing a long coat is standing near one of the bookshelves close to the exit. I've never seen him here before, and I don't remember seeing him come in.

What is he doing here?

I watch him grab a book from one of the shelves, tentatively flipping the pages one by one.

Until he lifts his head and looks me directly in the eyes.

I freeze, my heart beating in my throat, as I realize he's the same man who's been watching me from the bench across the street from my house. The same man I saw from the parking lot the other day. I thought I was losing it … and now, he's here, right in front of me, in the flesh.

Looking straight at me with those hauntingly blue eyes.

I grip the desk tight, feeling like it's the only thing tethering me to this world.

I swallow away the lump in my throat as he reaches into his pocket and takes out something small. I can't see what it is, but he places it inside the book and puts it back on the shelf.

After one last glance at me, he turns around and leaves.

I don't stop staring until he's left the building and is completely out of sight.

The door is still swinging back and forth, which is exactly how my heart feels right now.

For a while, I stay put, wondering if he's going to

return, but as the people come and go, none of them are him. People hand me their books, and I scan them while vaguely being aware of them standing in front of me. I feel like a ghost. One woman even snaps her fingers at me as if she's trying to wake me up.

I rush through the line as quickly as I can until the last customer has left with her books. When I finally gather enough courage, I peel myself away from my desk and stroll to the shelf in question. My fingers glide along the familiar books until they find an anomaly. One spine pushed in a little too far.

I grab it and take it out. I touch the front and back to make sure nothing's changed. It's a hardcopy of *Gone Girl*. I flip it open and sift through the pages until I find a thicker bit. There, I find a piece of paper.

Taking it out, I go through all the pages to make sure nothing else is inside and then place the book back on its shelf.

With the paper in my hand, I look around the library to see if anyone's noticed me. I don't know what's written on this paper, but I don't want to share it with anyone either. For some reason, it feels like this is a secret between us. A silent agreement to keep things hidden. And I don't want people to know this; least of all at the place I call 'work.'

So I turn my back against the big hall and unfold the paper.

It's a typed out message.

***

DRAKE

This is a story about a young woman and the man who couldn't take his eyes off her.

She's small and fragile like a lonely flower in a field weathering a strong wind. Her black hair tickles the back of her neck. She walks down the steps of her home with apprehension and haste. Something's bothering her, and I can see from the way she clutches her purse she knows…

I'm watching her.

I know what I'm doing is wrong.

But I can't stop myself … I want her so badly.

She's the type of girl no one sees. She can vanish in a crowd, and no one would come looking. No one would know she's gone missing. No one would care.

But I would.

I'm that man … the man who stalks because he's afraid of what will happen when he decides to pounce. Because he secretly desires the forbidden. To run his fingers through her smooth, silky hair. To touch her naked skin.

But he also knows … she does not want him.

This man is undesirable, a freak, because he follows and stares, watches and listens … instead of starting a conversation.

This man is not someone you want to be with.

A man who desires a woman he can't have only wants one thing ...

To stop her from being with someone else.

She's so beautiful ... he imagines wrapping his fingers around her neck, one by one, until nothing but his love is left.

***

Hyun

My body feels numb and cold to the bone.

I'm trembling. Not because of the goose bumps scattering over my skin, but because of what this message means.

Is it a threat or a tale of admiration?

I can't tell ... because I don't know for sure if this is about me.

But who else could it be for?

He looked directly at me, so I must be the girl in the story, right?

However, those last few words ... make me imagine fingers squeezing my throat. A tight, suffocating hold only committed to robbing me of my life. An attempt previously made by a man I hated from the very first moment I met him.

Gregory Warren.

I wince at the thought and tuck the note into my pocket, realizing what this could mean.

I'm insane for even keeping it—instead of shredding it—but I can't risk anyone finding this, even in tiny pieces. Not when my safety is at stake.

However … what's to say this note didn't come from Greg?

Maybe he got someone else to deliver it to me. Someone who stalks me day in, day out.

It's odd, you know. To read the words you experienced only months before.

Makes you wonder if your stalker was there to witness the whole ordeal.

3

"A Reflection" by Trent Reznor & Atticus Ross

Hyun

6 months before

I'm reading the newspaper while walking to work as I always do. With my favorite coffee from Starbucks in one hand and the newspaper in the other, I pass through the crowds of people on the way. It's funny, thinking about it, that I drink coffee from Starbucks while going to work at a coffee shop ... that is not Starbucks.

I guess my preference for another brand of coffee really doesn't support my case when I told my employer I wanted to work at his place. Really, I wanted to work there because I just needed a job badly, but he didn't need to know that.

Of course, I didn't think I'd get the job. I hadn't landed any of the others when I'd applied. Luckily, he hired me, and now, here I am … a barista for a few years now. I know it's not the greatest job in the world, but it's something. It pays well, so I'm happy. Besides, my co-workers are really nice, and I like them.

Plus, my boss let me take a few weeks off for that wicked game that Max Marino invited me to … not that I needed the time, since I left early.

I take a sip from my cup and enjoy the taste of cinnamon as I walk along the sidewalk while keeping my head down. I don't look at people and try not to draw any attention to myself. I don't want people to notice me. I'd rather disappear.

I know people out there are watching me … other than my stalker.

More specifically … one man and his wife.

Max Marino, the most powerful banker I've ever met, once wanted me, along with nine other girls. And now that I've stepped out of that wicked game, I know they're watching my every move … waiting for me to open my mouth. And I just know it won't end well for me if I do.

I have to be cautious. I don't want to give them any reason to kill me because I know he'd do it in a heartbeat if he so desired.

For that reason, I read the newspaper too. I'm searching for more information about them, anything.

News. Updates. Any information to make me believe they've finally settled down and will leave me in peace.

But the only bit of information I've uncovered since I left is who became his wife, and I expected no one less.

I sigh as I finish reading the front page. Nothing.

Maybe it means they're not interested in making their life public. Or maybe things really have settled down now that the game is over.

One thing's for sure, though … I will probably never feel safe again.

Especially not when I meet *him*.

I never thought I'd come face to face with the devil … and I never, ever imagined myself bumping into him and spilling my coffee all over his gray Armani suit.

"Watch it!" he yells.

"Oh, god," I mutter, looking up into his dark, cold eyes. "I'm sorry."

He pats his suit, huffing and puffing, his face red from annoyance.

I find myself enraptured by his presence. Not because he looks sleek with his black hair greased back, or because of the tiny gray hair I see dangling behind his ear, or because of the trimmed mustache above his thin lips.

No, it's because of the sheer dominance he exudes.

"I'm so sorry," I repeat, and I rummage through my purse to grab a tissue. "Here." I try to pat him down, but he snatches it from my hand and wipes himself with it.

"Thanks," he says with a gruff voice.

"I didn't see you. I don't know why. I should've looked up. Does it hurt? The coffee was scorching hot."

"No, it's fine," he says, this time showing a tentative smile. "Do you have more tissues, though?"

"Of course." I nod. Searching around in my bag, I find another pack and hand it to him. He pulls all of them out and pats himself down a few more times before discarding them into the bushes, just like that.

I contemplate going after them to throw them in the trash, but his eyes make me freeze.

"Where were you going? You seemed in a hurry," he says.

"Uh … work," I mutter, blushing a little.

It feels so awkward to talk to the stranger I just poured my coffee over. I look at my cup, which is now half-empty, and I wonder if it's okay to drink a sip. It's like it's tainted or something.

Suddenly, he sticks out his hand and says, "Gregory Warren."

"Uh …" I reluctantly take his hand. "Hyun Song."

He looks at my half-empty cup. "Let me buy you a new one."

"What?" My jaw drops a little, and I quickly take back my hand. "Oh, no. I ruined your suit. I should pay for you."

"No," he says with a stern voice. "I insist. After all

... your coffee is ruined too."

"It's okay. You don't—"

"I want to," he interrupts, and he steps closer, coming into my space.

I instinctively lean back. "I'm fine ... thank you. I need to get to work."

His eyes narrow as if he's checking me out, trying to spot a lie, but it's the honest to god truth.

"Well, then ... let me give you my number." He quickly fishes a card from his pocket and stuffs it into my hand, wrapping both of his hands around mine like he's trying to force me to keep it. He creepily leans in and whispers, "Call me."

I shudder, my lips quivering, and I pull my hand from his grip, turn around, and run.

I don't know what incited my response.

Why I chose to flee instead of say goodbye.

But one thing I do know for sure ... I never want to see him again.

***

Accompanying Song: "Logos" by Ludovico Einaudi

Now

I shoot up from my chair, dropping the book I was reading to the floor. I immediately grab the gun I tucked behind a vase in the corner of my room. My lungs fill with air as I take huge breaths, following my realization that it was just a dream. Still, I can't help but point the gun in every direction in my own home … worried someone might have snuck in.

Someone who wants to hurt me.

For a few seconds, I stand in the middle of my living room and listen to the sound of my own heartbeat. The sole clock hanging on the wall is a solemn reminder of the silence surrounding me … comforting me with the idea that nothing is wrong. Everything is as it should be.

I close my eyes and take a deep breath.

Calm down.

I tell myself this over and over until my heart no longer beats out of my chest. Then I lower the gun and put it back behind the vase. I walk to the kitchen to boil some water so I can make some much-needed tea. Rubbing my forehead, I try to push the memories from my head, reminding myself they were only dreams … and dreams can't hurt you.

Suddenly, I hear a ticking noise in the back of the room.

Not the ticking of the clock … but ticking against the window.

As the water begins to boil, I slowly tread toward the sound. My heart races and my legs quake once again, but I continue. I want to know what it is, even if it kills me. So with trembling fingers, I grasp the curtains and jerk them aside.

The ticking stops.

Nothing's there.

Not a bird in the tree.

Not a soul on the street.

I stare at the road for a few seconds, and I honestly wonder if I'm starting to lose my mind.

Frowning, I turn and shut the curtains again.

Only to hear the ticking begin again.

My eyes twitch, and I march toward the front door, yanking it open like I've got beef with someone. Maybe I do, or maybe this is the stupidest thing I've ever done … but I'm doing it anyway.

I walk to the other side of my house where the ticking on the window occurred, but I don't see anyone.

"Hello?" I call out. "Anyone there?"

Yeah, like that's going to work.

I check my surroundings, but no one appears from behind a bush or a tree. No one leaves their home. No one even replies.

See? I am losing my mind, after all.

But as I turn around … a peculiar scratch beneath my shoes compels me to look down.

Pebbles.

Ten, maybe fifteen, all right in front of my window.

My garden doesn't have any pebbles.

I pick one up and look at it as if it's going to tell me where it came from. The sound of an engine pulls my eyes away from the pebble and to the car driving past me. I glare at the driver to see if he gazes back. He doesn't.

I let out a long, drawn-out breath and tuck the pebble into my pocket, making my way back into my house. I slam the door shut behind me, hoping it can keep whatever's trying to come in out.

However, the moment I set foot on my carpet, I stop.

There's a red envelope on the floor.

Did I leave the door open?

I didn't close it.

Someone came in and left this here.

I immediately rush to the vase, pick up the gun again, and search the house. Sweat rolls down my back. One by one, I scan all the rooms, pulling up blankets and pushing aside curtains wherever I go. Leaving nothing the way it was. In the end, my house is a mess. But an empty, lonely mess with me as its sole occupant. Exactly how it should be.

I sigh and tuck the gun back behind the vase.

My attention focuses on the red envelope, which lies on the floor like a gift begging to be opened … and I just know I can't resist.

***

DRAKE

Hours before

Through a narrow gap in the curtains, I watch her.

She sits behind her vanity, looking at herself in the mirror as she paints a thin black line along the top edges of her eyes. The way she elegantly yet carefully swipes the small brush along her eyelids has captured my attention, along with every other little detail. Her black hair floats in a gush of wind coming in through the window while her eyes remain fixated on the mirror and her fingers finish the lines gently. She's poised. Sophisticated in her movements. Perfectly beautiful in her lonely existence.

A perfect victim for my crude desires.

I know it's wrong to desire her.

To watch her from the window ... or all the way from my car, where she can't even see me because my windows are tinted black.

Just as black as my heart ...

I clutch my chest as I think about her. Day and night.

Her entire existence consumes me to the point of wanting her so badly I'd kill myself if I couldn't come close.

I'm dangerous. The worst kind of enemy to cross your path.

But as unlikely as it seems, I'm not the bad guy in this story.

I'm the one who wants to give her everything she needs. The one who wants to *take* her and lock her up where no one can find her.

I watch her every morning … while she drinks her favorite coffee from Starbucks as she reads the newspaper all by herself, the ticking clock on the wall her only companion.

At night, I peek through the small gap in her curtains hanging from her window and admire her in her sleep. She's half-naked, wearing only a small green bralette and matching lace panties. My hand reaches for the window, and I let my fingers slide down across the cold glass, wondering if she'll notice I'm here.

I know she knows.

I've seen her look at me from her window.

I watched her pick up the notes I left for her.

I hope she likes them.

She wrestles with the blanket, the nightmares from her past clearly occupying her. But as her face contorts and her sweet, wet lips purse, I find myself so … fucking … aroused.

I don't know if it's the desperate look on her face or my fucked-up mind … but I want her so badly.

I start touching myself.

Right in front of her window.

In the middle of the night.

I zip down my pants and take out my rock-hard cock, stroking it from top to bottom. Seeing her while she doesn't even know I'm here only makes it more exciting. More wrong.

And nothing gratifies me more.

I've never done this.

Jerked myself off to the thought of a girl I can't have. A girl who isn't even awake to know I'm here, lurking on the other side of the windows.

I'm a motherfucking creep, and I know it … but I don't give a damn.

She's too beautiful, too innocent, too lovely not to desire.

Too fucking perfect not to taint.

I know what I'm doing is wrong, but I still do it.

I keep rubbing myself until the veins in my cock bulge and pulse with greed. I lick my lips at the sight of her furrowed brows and her fingers clutching her blanket as I imagine lying there, holding her down while I fuck her brains out.

I wish to fuck out her innocence.

Watch those pretty little lips part in euphoric bliss as I make her come like no other man ever has.

I want to see the lights in her eyes snuff out.

I want to watch it all.

In the dark of the night, I silently come, jetting my seed all over her window, right where her body lies in view.

It feels so fucking good to release all that pent-up lust. And even though it satiates me to some extent, I'm still not completely satisfied. Something's missing. Something tangible.

Her body ... a response to my actions ...

Something.

But she continues to sleep ... as she should.

I grab some tissues from my pocket and wipe the cum off her window then tuck my cock back into my pants. I turn around, and after one final glance, I leave, never to return.

Or so I say.

Telling myself that is the only way I can accept my own deviance.

Of course, I know it's a lie.

And she knows it too.

***

Hyun

Now

My fingers tremble as they hold the note. The story I just read … a man touching himself as he watches me through my window …

It made my thighs clench.

I stop reading and feel my own pussy thump between my legs.

What is wrong with me?

Biting my lip, I stare at the words, repeating them over and over in my head. I wonder when this happened. Was it today? Yesterday? Days or weeks ago? And could I have noticed if I'd only woken up?

Someone's watching me. Relishing in my privacy. Fantasizing about my body. Even touching himself while looking at me …

It's wrong, so wrong.

But then why … why do I feel so excited that I'd want to touch myself too?

Don't lose yourself in the moment.

I suck in a breath and lift my head. If he dropped

38

this note here just now, he must be close. So I turn around, open the front door, and stare outside.

A navy blue car sits on the corner of the street, one that looks the same as what Greg drives.

But as I stare at it, its tires screech, and it shoots away around the corner.

4

Accompanying Song: "Daydream" by Ruelle

Hyun

The next day

I walk around the outside my house and check all the windows. I see nothing peculiar, which makes me wonder if anything really happened ... or if it was all a lie on that piece of paper. But then, when I get to my bedroom window, I notice a white smudge dripping down.

I take a tissue from my pocket to wipe it away ... and I notice it sticks.

I look at it for a few seconds, trying to come to terms with the fact that he sprayed his cum on my window. I feel strange. Like he's watching me again ...

like he's obsessed.

But for some odd reason, I'm not even mad. I'm actually amazed. Amazed that he watches me in my sleep without regret, without restraint. That he'd go so far as to come all over my window and not give a shit about me finding it.

It's as if he wants me to know how badly he wants me.

Like he's marking my house.

Marking *me* … as his.

A shiver runs up and down my body, but it isn't from fear. It's from excitement.

Maybe I am really losing my mind.

***

5.5 months before

I drive as fast as I can, realizing I'm already too late for my own birthday party. I knew I should've gone home sooner, but the customers just kept pouring into the coffee shop. Well, nothing to do about it now because I can't turn back time.

I park my car on the driveway and jump out, quickly locking it as I walk to the front door of my parents' home. We're celebrating it there since I'm a little lonely in my own home. Besides, they wanted to organize something special for me, so I appreciate the gesture.

Although it is very unusual for my parents because they don't normally do this kind of thing ... they're normally only busy with themselves. They always badger me about my education and about whether I've found a better job. I'm sure they'll do that exact same thing now too, but I just ignore it.

I ring the doorbell, and my mom opens it with a big smile.

"Hyun! Finally," Mom says in Korean. She grabs me by the arm and pulls me inside. "I thought you'd make us wait forever."

"Sorry," I say. "I ran a little late because of work."

"You mean that coffee shop you work at?" She takes my coat.

"Yeah, had a busy day."

She sighs. "Hyun, when are you going to find a better job?"

I roll my eyes. "Not now, Mom ... please."

She shrugs. "Well, you can't keep doing this."

"It's my birthday, Mom. Let's celebrate, okay?" I give her a smile in an attempt to defuse the situation.

"Fine ..." She walks past me and goes to the kitchen.

A crowd meets me and stops me from following her. Everyone wants to shake my hand. Uncles, aunts, distant cousins. They're all here, and I've not seen them in ages. It's funny how fast time goes when you have a job and are trying to make something of your life. You often forget about things like this.

My mom suddenly appears from the crowd with a piece of cake. "Happy birthday!" She kisses me on the cheeks and pushes the plate into my hand. "Enjoy."

"Thanks, Mom," I say, greedily taking a bite.

"Your gift is waiting for you at the table," she says, winking and gesturing for me to follow her.

Frowning, I look up and walk with her, wondering what she means.

But then I see a man in a suit standing at the table with his back toward us ... and the moment he turns around, I almost drop the cake.

"Hello, Hyun."

It's Gregory Warren.

His voice sends a cold shiver down my spine. "Happy birthday."

"Gregory ..." I shift back to speaking English.

"Call me Greg," he says, grabbing my free hand to kiss the back.

I quickly take it back and wipe it on my shirt. "What are you doing here?"

"He's a guest, sweetie, be nice," my mom sneers in her best English. "I invited him."

"How—"

"We know each other from work," my father interjects, patting Gregory on the back of the shoulder. "He's actually my boss, but we consider each other friends. Right, Greg?"

"But ... I thought you worked ..."

"At the biggest bank in town, remember?" Dad says. "Are you all right, honey?"

No. I'm not all right.

I feel sick to my stomach, but I won't tell them that.

"Let me take that for you …" Greg takes the plate of cake from my hand and places it on the table behind him. Then he grabs both my hands and says, "You look like you could use some good news."

"I'm fine," I say, trying to pull my hands from his, but he won't let go.

He leans in and sniffs awkwardly. "You smell like … coffee."

"I work at a coffee shop," I reply, finally managing to pull my hands from his grip.

"Oh … No wonder. I'm sure you could use a jumpstart, don't you?"

"What?" I frown. "I love my job."

"Of course, you do." He folds his arms. "But maybe I can fix you up with a better job … What do you think about being a bank employee?"

"A bank employee?" I make a face. "No, thanks."

"Aww … well, what about …" He mulls it over for a second, rubbing his chin. "I know!" He snaps his fingers. "What about a librarian?"

"Librarian? Where'd you get that from?" I ask.

"Oh, yes!" Mom squeals. "You like books, right?"

"Um … yeah, but—" I mutter.

"It's a step up from being a barista," Dad says.

44

"I personally know the head librarian at the local library here in town, so he and I can have a quick chat. I can get you the job easily," Greg says with a smirk. "Interested?"

My dad throws his arm over my shoulder and pulls me in for a close hug. "Of course, she is. Right, honey?" He gazes at me. "This is one opportunity you don't want to miss."

I know what my parents want.

I also know this sounds too good to be true.

Yes, I love books and reading. Of course, I'd love to work in a place where they can surround me all day long. If only it didn't feel so damn wrong. Like a lie I just can't believe. Why would he pick me?

"She'll take you up on the offer," my mom suddenly says, grabbing Greg's arm as if it seals the deal. "You're so kind."

"Oh, it's my pleasure." Greg gloats. "I want only the best for my friends ... and their beautiful daughter." His eyes are like those of a hawk, honing in on me like prey.

"Greg is such a nice young man, don't you agree?" my mom asks me gleefully.

With furrowed brows, I answer, "I guess ..."

"Hyun ..." Dad murmurs.

"Don't worry. She'll get used to me," Greg says, chuckling.

Slowly, but surely, it begins to dawn on me.

My eyes widen, and my jaw drops.

"You know, Greg's still on the market," Mom whispers.

She doesn't need to tell me. I already know.

Just like I know why he was invited. Why my parents lured me here. Why I was suddenly offered a job. And why my parents seem so fond of this creepy man who is anything but young compared to me.

They want me to be his.

"No ..." I say, soft, but sternly.

My parents look at me as if they just saw a ghost. "What did you say, honey?" Dad asks.

"I said no."

My mom cocks her head, and the confused look on her face suddenly changes to cold-hearted rage. "You will do what he says. We've already made up our minds."

"What?" I cringe.

My father swallows and looks me directly in the eye. "We think Greg is a suitable match."

I shake my head. I can't believe this is happening. Can't believe this is real.

"No ..."

"It's not up to you," Mom says.

The dreaded word slips from her lips. *Seon.* The Korean word for arranged marriage.

They say arranged marriages don't exist in the modern world, but people are wrong. It happens every day, even in the most civilized countries. And now, it's happening to me.

Tears well up in my eyes. "So you're saying I have no say in my own life?"

They remain as rigid as I remember them to be whenever they're angry. Their only interest in my life has been how they could make me the star of the family. The proud asset. A girl who would do their bidding and give them everything they wanted. Like a mountain of gold they could sit on, easily persuaded to do anything to get their hands on more, more, more. And now, they've found a way.

"Honey, we think this is in your best interest."

"No!"

All the guests have turned quiet, and I can feel their eyes pierce my back.

"Let me do the talking …" Greg says, and he tries to approach me. "Listen … Hyun … we both like each other. Let's not make this any more difficult."

"You can't be serious …" I look at my parents, and I see my mother's hand disappear into her pockets. She's touching something inside, I can see it, and it can only mean one thing.

Money.

Tears run down my cheeks as I shake my head and scream, "I thought you loved me."

"We do, honey. We love you so, so much. That's why we think you'll be great with Greg."

"*Don't* say that!" I yell. "I've never had a worse birthday in my entire life," I say, turning around and walking away.

"Hyun ..."

Mom throws some Korean swear words at me while I run up the stairs, but I block everything out.

For now, I'll hide in my old room for as long as I can. Once all the guests have left, I can run down and escape too. I won't let him have me. I can't let it happen.

I rush in and slam the door shut. My mom bangs on it, but I don't open up. I walk backward until my back hits the wall, where I sink to my knees and cuddle myself, letting my tears run free.

I feel weak, vulnerable, afraid.

And this door is my only protection against him and my family as they barter me off like goods.

***

Accompanying Song: "Logos" by Ludovico Einaudi

Now

The water from the shower rushes down my face. I try to forget the memories clouding my mind, but they keep coming back to the forefront. It often happens when I'm home alone.

I tell myself it's in the past. That I'm still here, alive.

But it doesn't take away the pain inside my heart.

What my parents did to me was the pinnacle of

their greed. All those years they used me for their own gain—and then gave me away to a man I didn't even know. That was the icing on the cake.

But that was then, and this is now.

I take a deep breath and close my eyes, letting my mouth catch the warm water.

Suddenly, I hear a clicking noise.

My eyes open wide, water still gushing down, and I turn off the faucet and listen.

No more clicking, but I swear I heard something, so I grab a towel and wrap it around my body as I step out of the shower. The first thing I do is walk to my kitchen and take a knife from the drawer. Then I search my house, yelling, "Hello? Is anyone there?"

No response.

Of course, not. It's all in my head.

Still, I check all the rooms in the house until I've confirmed I'm alone.

But then I reach the front door … and I twist the handle, opening it without much trouble.

I forgot to lock it.

My hand instinctively covers my mouth as it slowly opens wide, creaking loudly. Something tickles beneath my feet. A chill runs up and down my spine the moment I look down and see an envelope lying on the floor.

I pick it up and look around the neighborhood. I don't even care that a passerby walking her dog sees me in only a towel. I smile and wave awkwardly, which only increases her pace.

I grab the door handle and pull back, allowing it to close. The sound of it reverberates in my ears … the same clicking noise I heard when I was in the shower.

Someone was here.

5

Accompanying Song: "Hungry Like The Wolf" by Snow Hill

DRAKE

From the living room, I can hear the shower running. I step closer to the only light source in the house, my heart practically beating out of my chest from excitement. She's so close; I could almost taste her. I could almost take her.

I shouldn't.

Yet I can't stop myself from inching closer with every passing second.

It's as if my feet gravitate toward her. My mind can no longer stop my body from approaching, even if it's wrong on all levels.

I watch her shower. Through the curtains, I can see

the silhouette of her body, and sometimes, her skin peeks through the gap. Her body looks like silk, so smooth. Her olive skin so deliciously appetizing, I want to lick it.

I stop myself before I go too far.

I already went past the moral line when I came all over her window.

Standing near the door to her bathroom, I admire her from a distance, listening to the water cascading down her skin. She massages herself with oils, and the scent is intoxicating. I feel the warmth prickle on my skin, and at this moment, I wonder if she'll ever want me.

If it'd ever be okay to talk to her.

To touch her.

To be with her.

The more I watch her, the more I want from her. I'm physically incapable of staying away. I feel my best when I'm close to her. I only desire to give her everything she needs. I don't want to hurt her, yet I know she has every reason to fear me.

She's fragile. Emotionally drained. Used.

Smacked around like a wet rag by a man who didn't know his own strength.

Her man.

He likes beating things senseless. It makes him feel powerful. Better than her.

Calling the cops is useless; they're in his pocket, and she knows that too. That's why she never did a thing to stop it. That's why she ran away from him.

She ran and ran …

But both of us know you can never run away from a lie.

∗∗∗

Accompanying Song: "Violent Delights Have Violent Ends" by Ramin Djawadi

Hyun

The note ends suddenly. It's the first handwritten one, but the letters aren't normal; they're blocky. And the final words seem scratchy … like they ended swiftly because he had to go. As if he realized the longer he stayed, the bigger the chance of his discovery.

I shiver and swallow as I realize he was there the whole time I was naked and didn't say a word.

If I'd known he was there …

I don't even want to think about it.

But still … his comment about not being able to call the cops is too close for comfort.

I feel like he knows more than he's letting on. Like he's been watching me longer than I thought. And it irks me … because he's right.

When I first called 911 and the cops came to my house, Greg sweet-talked them into forgetting the whole thing ever happened. He made them believe I was lying. That I was upset because of a fight and didn't mean to keep them busy. They believed him, and not just that … when they were gone, Greg told me they'd never listen to me. He'd bought them all off. And he said if I ever called them again, I'd be sorry. Just like that, my life was no longer safe. No longer my own. That night … he even forced me to lay down on his lap so he could spank me until my skin was blood red.

I shake my head and force the memories from my head. I will not give him power over me anymore. My self-worth is my own, and no one can touch that.

Someone wants to send me messages? Fine. I'll keep them. Besides, I don't have anything else to lose. I don't feel threatened. I know what that feels like because I lived it for months, but this … this is something different.

In a weird way, I'm flattered someone would go through this much trouble to be with me. Even going so far as to enter my home without my knowledge. Yet he still hasn't made a move. All he's done is watch me … and I don't know why, but the thought doesn't even creep me out anymore. I don't think he really wants to harm me. It sounds more like a deep-seated need to be with me.

So I take the note with me and place it on the stack I've collected. Then I grab a folder and stuff them all inside so I can keep them together. I won't throw them out. I won't show them to the police. I want to see where this trail of crumbs leads. Even if it's dangerous or bad... I don't care. Why? Because it's my choice. The one and only choice in my life I've made by myself.

Besides, these notes might be useful ... one day.

***

A few days later

As I walk out the door to go on a morning jog, I notice a second car parked in my driveway, and it isn't mine.

I stop and pull my earbuds from my ears, the music still ringing as I stare at the car in front of me.

"Morning!"

I look up and see my next-door neighbor Lorelei watering her plants. She smiles and waves with soil-covered hands, so I smile back and say, "Good morning."

"Got some visitors?"

I frown. "Why do you ask?"

"Oh, I just thought ... well, looking at the car, I figured you and Greg might be back together again."

My heart stops beating for a second, and I vehemently shake my head.

"Oh … But … what's his car doing there then?"

For a second, I'm surprised she knows what his car looks like, but then I remember showing her a few pictures that I carried in my wallet just so she'd know who to look for if he came back to get me.

"I don't know …" I sigh and look around, but I don't see anyone except us.

Lorelei puts down her rake and says, "Now that I think about it, I did see someone when I walked into my shed a half-hour ago to grab some tools. Some guy wearing a hoodie and a long coat. He went into the forest behind our homes."

My lips part, but I don't know what to say. All I can do is hope that it wasn't Greg.

"Maybe it was him," she adds, only unnerving me more.

I nod and take a deep breath. "Thanks." I turn around and start walking to the forest.

"Are you going to follow him?"

"Yes."

"Good luck." I hear Lorelei's voice behind me, but I no longer respond.

My heart is racing, and my head is too busy trying to make sense of this. Trying not to panic.

If Greg is really out there … what is he doing here? I have to know if it's him.

Despite being scared shitless, I still tread through

the fallen leaves and over the rotting branches, making my way through the dense forest. The sky almost seems pitch-black from here, as if the day has suddenly turned to night.

A twig snaps underneath my foot, and then I hear a rustling noise in front of me.

I rush past the trees and come to an open area with a small pool of water in the middle. "Is anyone there?" I call out, my voice hampering. Fading into nothingness.

The light hooting of a bird, possibly an owl, is my only response.

However, something peculiar draws my attention. A string hangs from a low branch of a tree on the other side of the pool. Before I do anything, I look around and check if anyone's there, but I don't see a soul or hear a thing.

Maybe he's already long gone.

I walk around it and approach the string, only to discover another note dangling from it. For some reason, the fact another note is waiting to be found makes me less fearful. I tear it off carefully and read the typed out words.

Are you ready to play?

I check the back, but it's blank. There's only this

one line ... and it makes the hairs on the back of my neck stand up straight.

Am I ready to play?

That depends on the game.

I smirk and tuck the note into my pocket. That's when I hear rustling behind me, and I turn around and run toward the sound. I swear I could see something disappearing behind a tree, but as I approach, I find it's nothing more than a cute squirrel jumping up into the tree.

I blow out a breath and smile to myself. No need to be on edge.

Except ... when I hear the humming of an engine and the loud screeching of a car racing away.

***

Accompanying Song: "Obsession" by Golden State (Animotion Cover)

DRAKE

With my Polaroid on the passenger's seat, I race off in my car, making sure to stay low so no one can see me. I know her neighbor saw me, but my hoodie hid my face, so I doubt she knows who I am.

As I hit the gas and turn the corner with one hand,

I sift through the photos I took of Hyun with my other hand. Some of them show her looking up at books in the library. A few others are of her picking up my various notes. Every time, the look on her face is what captures most of my attention. That, and the blush ... god, that fucking blush.

With one hand, I unbutton my pants and dive in while the other stays firmly on the wheel. While I look through the photos one by one, I focus on her mouth and picture myself running the tip of my cock along her pouty lips. I'm already hard from just the thought, and I stroke myself long and slowly. I want to take my time to enjoy these pictures, and I really don't care if anyone catches me jerking off in my own car right now. I don't even care that I'm still cruising down the street; I just want to touch myself while I look at her.

I like her too much. So much so that I can't stop thinking about her. Her presence consumes my every fucking thought. I won't be able to hold back much longer ... and I doubt she'll want me to by the time she realizes what I could do to her body.

6

"A Reflection" by Trent Reznor & Atticus Ross

Hyun

5 months before

I've worked day in and day out, trying to keep myself occupied. I even asked my boss for extra hours, just to stay here. He agreed, but only if I did it for free, which I do. I don't care about it. I'm doing anything to avoid having to go back home, where I know that man will be waiting for me.

He followed me everywhere.

When I finally managed to escape my parents' home after the party, he was on my porch the next day, stepping foot on my lawn. No matter how many times I told him no, he wouldn't listen. It got so bad he even tried to force me to go with him, blocking my way with his car.

I won't let it happen, so I've kind of disappeared now, for the time being.

My parents have tried to call me a gazillion times, probably to ask me where I am and to tell me to get home immediately. After a while, I turned off my phone and just ignored it all. But I know he's out there somewhere, waiting for me. And when he finds me, I know it'll be too late to escape.

I can't let that happen, so I've been sleeping in the back of the coffee shop for a few days now, behind a few boxes where I've made a bed out of coffee bean bags and cartons. I keep sneaking in through the back door whenever it's time to lock up. No one notices I'm gone … not many people do anyway. My boss doesn't know about it, luckily, because I'm sure he'd kick me out if he did.

A new customer making his way to the front of the line pulls me from my thoughts.

Sighing, I hand the cup of cappuccino to him and say, "Have a pleasant day, sir."

He gazes down at his cup. "I didn't order this …"

For a moment, I'm flabbergasted, and then I realize he ordered a Frappuccino. "I'm so sorry, sir."

He hands the cup back to me, and I quickly dump it and begin again. As I give him the proper coffee, my boss stands behind me and says, "I know you asked for more hours, but if you're gonna mess it up, that's not very useful."

"I know. I'm sorry. It won't happen again," I say.

"Really?" He raises his brows at me.

"Promise," I add, and I give him a fake smile.

"All right. If you say so." He places his hand on my shoulder. "Your next customer is here. I'm gonna go back to my office to get some of that paperwork done. If you need any help, holler, all right? Good luck."

I don't reply because when I look up and see *him* standing in front of me, I freeze.

Out of all people, it has to be him.

Gregory Warren.

How did he find out where I worked? I never told him the exact location.

And how did he know I was here today? Never once did I tell him my schedule.

"Hello, Hyun. What a pleasure to see you again …" The wretched smile on his face makes my eyes watery.

There's only one thing I can say. "Leave."

"Now, now, is that the way to speak to a customer?" He cocks his head. "Maybe I should speak to the manager about your behavior toward me."

"No," I say sternly.

"Hyun?" I hear behind me, and when I glance over my shoulder, I see my manager appear from the back. "What's this about?"

"Oh, Hyun and I are practically family, and I wanted to speak with her for a second, but she says she's got so much work she can't take a minute break,"

Greg fills in. It's as if he's played it all out in his head. Lie after lie.

"It's fine. I'll take over for her," my manager says.

"But—"

"No buts. You go take a break, Hyun. You obviously need it." My manager pushes me out in front of the counter, closer to Greg. "Go on," he spurs.

Greg wraps his filthy fingers around my shoulder and pulls me so close I can smell his stench, making bile rise in my throat. "Yeah, c'mon, Hyun. We're gonna have a little chat."

"Please don't …" I mutter, tears rolling down my cheeks.

"Honey, you know this has been a long time coming."

"I don't want you," I whisper, hoping the customers don't hear. I don't want to lose my job. It's the only thing I like about my life. The only thing I chose for myself. The only part I have control over.

"But I want *you*," he murmurs, smiling sickly. "My wife."

Those words create goose bumps all over my body.

"You have no choice in the matter. Your parents wanted money, and I wanted you. What's done is done. But I'll give you a good life." He grins, and I know it's a lie too.

He escorts me outside where his car is parked right in front of the door. "Get in."

He stands behind me and blocks my only way out. I

turn around and face him, looking directly into his eyes with fury.

He licks his lips. "You don't want to make a scene, Hyun … If you do, I'll make sure there isn't a coffee shop to return to when I'm done with you."

I shudder, and the tears stop immediately. This monster deserves nothing.

I don't want to lose the only place that makes me feel like I actually own my own life.

I have no other choice but to step into the car.

So I turn around and crawl in quietly, realizing this might be the last time I set foot on the ground as a free woman.

***

Accompanying Song: "Daydream" by Ruelle

4 months before

In my white gown, I walk along the aisle, tears staining my eyes. Still, I refuse to cry. I hold my breath as I lay my eyes on the man in the suit inches away from me, his wicked smile crushing my soul.

Every step I take is another one toward being a prisoner in a loveless marriage, and each of them feels heavier … more painful than I could ever imagine.

I stay silent through most of the ordeal. I'm only

partially there; my mind has already long drifted off to a place where I can be at peace. He holds my hand like it already belongs to him, and when I'm asked for my answer, I simply answer yes.

A ring that feels cold and unwelcome slips on my finger, and Greg leans in for the most hideous kiss I've ever felt. My life, stolen away by a madman.

When everything is over, we walk out through the rows of people, and I'm overcome with shame at having to look into their eyes, knowing it's all a lie. My parents seem joyful, smiling brightly as I pass them. Money is all it took to make them happy, in exchange for my own happiness.

Mom briefly grabs my hand and squeezes. "I'm so proud of you, honey."

Her words sound hollow, only adding to the chasm slowly eating away my heart.

It all seems like a blur. Minutes and seconds merge until I don't even know how much time has passed or how late it is.

When the guests congratulate us on our marriage, I manage to slip outside with a glass of champagne and drink it outside on a bench. I'm on my own for the first time in a long while. Greg probably lets me out of his sight because he knows I can no longer escape him.

This ring ...

I stare at it, wishing I could toss it away.

It burns into my skin.

I look up and wipe away the tears I promised I

wouldn't cry.

In the distance, a man walks away over a dirt path as he pulls his hoodie over his head. For a moment, he glances at me over his shoulder and shows a tiny hint of a smile.

After which he disappears.

***

"A Reflection" by Trent Reznor & Atticus Ross

Now

My fingers glide over the ring on my finger, twisting and turning it until I can't feel it anymore. I look at the notes I received so far. I've read them so many times I can almost recite them word for word without looking.

I don't know why, but these notes … they feel … like they're important. Personal. Meaningful. Unlike Greg.

He never wrote anything. He always called people on the phone instead of sending messages. And if it was really him, wanting me back, I'd guess he'd barge down my door right about now. He wouldn't go about it in a sneaky way.

No, this is someone else.

I fumble with my ring again, and it bothers me so much that I pull it off and toss it away.

It's the first time I've taken it off since my wedding, and damn, does it feel liberating. I don't even know why it took me so long to take it off in the first place. Maybe I kept it on out of habit. A silent reminder of his chokehold on me.

But enough is enough.

I get up and put the notes back into the folder. However, as I lean over my table, I notice something in the trashcan next to my door.

Frowning, I walk over to it and pluck out a half-smoked cigarette.

For a few seconds, I stare at it, wondering what it's doing here.

I don't smoke.

Rage boils up from deep inside, and I crush the cigarette in my hand. Then I grab the gun that I hid behind the vase and tuck it into my pocket. Anger blinds me from making the right decision. Instead, I storm out of my house, jump into my car, and drive straight to Greg's.

For ages, I was fearful of going back and facing the beast, and still, the anxiety makes me tremble. However, the raging fury inside me has taken over, and it wants out. There's no stopping me. No matter how many times the voices in my head tell me it's a bad idea, I still go to his house, ignoring all the warnings I know are there for a reason.

I just have to know.

I don't just knock on his door. I practically ram it,

all while smashing the doorbell too. "Greg! I know you're in there!" I know it's evening, but at this point, I don't care if the neighbors hear me.

I slam his door a few more times and yell, "Greg! Open the door!"

After a while, I feel it move underneath my hand, and I step back.

He casually opens the door, staring at me with an uninterested look and an aloof attitude. "Hyun ... Finally come back, have you?"

I ignore his taunt. "You came into my house, didn't you?" I say, and I show him the cigarette, which I'd conveniently stuffed into my left pocket.

He narrows his eyes while looking at it then he focuses his attention on me. "Have you lost your mind?"

"I know you'd do anything to get me back," I reply.

"You stupid girl ... do you really think I'm that stupid? Causing a scene in front of your neighbors?"

"You have the police in your pocket. What's stopping you from breaking in and entering my home to steal me away again? It's not as if it stopped you before." I sneer.

"Not when people could call the news."

"Oh, so there is *something* that holds you back ... bad publicity." I scoff.

He sighs. "Did you just come here to accuse me of leaving a cigarette in your home?"

"Don't lie to me," I hiss.

He leans in and grabs my arm, his grip strong and painful. "Let's get one thing straight here," he mutters under his breath. "I'm only letting you live there because you made such a big deal about being separated from me. I'm trying to show you what a true gentleman I can be by giving you what you want. But don't … test … my … patience."

Each word comes out as a restrained yell.

"Let. Me. Go," I say, trying not to let my voice fluctuate.

I won't show him any weakness. I'm way past that point.

"Or what? You're going to call the cops? Last I checked, you came to *my* home."

I jerk free and take my gun from my right pocket, pointing it at him. "Stay back."

I walk backward as he holds up his hands. "No need for violence, Hyun."

"Shut up!" *Violence.* Like he doesn't know he's the violent one.

Manipulative bastard.

"I'm keeping an eye on you … Hyun." His voice is so low, so dark, that it makes my skin crawl.

He's a liar. A deceitful devil. One day … I'll prove it to the world.

"You can't keep running away from me," he adds.

"Don't try to stop me," I hiss, and I turn and run away, still clutching the gun.

Turmoil fills my head as I make my way back

home, barely able to keep my mind on the road. When I've finally parked my car in my driveway and get back inside, I sink to my knees against the door. I breathe in and out, but nothing I do slows the beating of my heart.

I scream and get up, marching toward the kitchen to grab a bottle of wine. I pull out the cork and drink from the bottle. I don't need a glass when I'm in this deep.

I spend the rest of the evening drinking and watching game shows on TV while trying to forget about this whole ordeal. I don't even care whether I get drunk or if it's bad or not. I need this. For just one moment, I'd like to forget all the bad stuff.

So I drink until I can no longer see straight, which is when I decide to go to bed.

Too bad I can't even walk without stumbling into everything.

And as I try to grab the empty bottle so I can throw it in the trash, I fall over my own feet and land headfirst on the table.

I black out.

I don't know for how long but, goddamn, does it hurt.

My head aches, and when I touch my forehead, it feels wet. When I bring my hand to look at it, I see blood.

But I'm too drunk to care. Too drunk to move. Too drunk to help myself.

And as I feel myself fade again, I hear a creaking noise and something tugs at my arm.

I don't know how much time passes before I come to my senses again.

But somehow, someway, I ended up in my bed with a Band-Aid over my wound. And with my clothes removed and wearing a fresh smelling nightgown.

I blink a couple of times to try to make sense of it all. I don't remember getting up or taking off my clothes.

That's when I notice a dark figure looming in the corner of my bedroom.

Part II
The Transformation

7

Accompanying Song: "Hungry Like The Wolf" by Snow Hill

DRAKE

I watch her wake up from across the room. She's been in and out of it for a while now, but her eyes haven't looked this sharp since. She's finally seemed to notice me.

I hold my breath and watch the shock seep into her veins.

It's strange to see her look at me like that. When we finally come face to face.

Maybe I shouldn't have stayed. Maybe I should've left. But that's not what I did.

I wanted to watch over her, take care of her, and make sure she's all right.

And she sure doesn't seem all right.

She clutches the blanket and pulls it up toward her neck, trying to hide the skin underneath. Then she looks down at her chest, and I know she realizes I changed her clothes.

I didn't do it to be a pervert, even though her body is a sight to behold. It's thrilling, but it's not what I get off on. I get off on her knowing I'm there, watching, fantasizing about her.

But this time ... she didn't even see me coming.

I admit breaking into a house isn't exactly something that can make a person trust you, but since the door wasn't locked, as usual, I just let myself in. I knew she'd do something she'd regret.

I've been watching her the entire day, following her wherever she went in my car, but when I saw her going to that man ... I knew she was in trouble. So I stayed with her and even sat down on a stone in her yard beneath her window to keep an eye on her all night. But then I heard a loud bang, so I went inside and found her lying on the floor with blood on her head.

Of course, my first instinct was to help her. Anyone would do that.

But it also gave me an excuse to stay with her. To be by her side like a bodyguard.

One who stalks her in the night.

I step toward her, and she swallows, clearly nervous. However, her vulnerable state only makes her that much more attractive. She *needs* me.

I lick my lips and say, "Did you read my notes?"

She nods softly, her skin tinted pink.

Her face is so pretty to look at up close. I miss it every second I'm not near her. I don't know why I'm so infatuated with her. I've never felt this way for a woman … Maybe it's because we share something no one else does. Something secret between us.

Or maybe it's because she was already taken … by a monster.

And I want her for myself.

I breathe through my nose and make a fist, forcing myself to turn away before I let it go too far.

"Where are you going?"

Her soft voice pulls my heartstrings.

With my hand on the doorjamb, I linger and wonder if I should stay.

"I can't stay …" I reply, my voice heavy and full of worries. "It isn't right."

And with those final words, I leave her home.

Talking isn't my thing anyway.

***

Hyun

I've been staring at the ceiling the entire night.

I didn't close a single eye. I couldn't sleep. Not with the thought of having him watching me from the corner or outside like he always does.

Should I be worried? Probably.

But he never came back. Even though I wished he would.

Because when I laid my eyes on him, I couldn't take them off him. My gaze was instantly locked on the piercing blue eyes hidden beneath thick brows, and even though most of his face hid behind a hoodie, I could still see the sharp features, the angles in his face, and his square jaw with a little bit of scruff. When he took a breath, the muscles in his chest tightened, and I could see each and every line. Like a sculpture so perfectly crafted.

So … sexy.

It's wrong, and I know it, but still … I can't stop myself from thinking exactly that.

I feel like I want to invite him in.

With him as a protector … I could definitely live.

It's nuts. Completely nuts. But I didn't even care that he'd changed my clothes for me and put me in bed. It didn't feel threatening. Granted, it was kind of strange to realize he'd done it after the fact. But it still doesn't feel … dangerous.

Greg is dangerous.

But with this guy … it's different.

One thing's for sure, though. I'm probably going to see more of him now.

The next morning, I get up with a pang in my stomach and a roaring headache, but I'm determined not to let my mistake from last night ruin the rest of my day.

So I drink a glass of water and put on my sweatpants to go outside. After all, I have a mailbox to check.

With a stupid smile on my face, I open my door and traipse outside in my flip-flops to check the mailbox. And just as I expected, a note is stuck inside. The sight of it excites me. I don't know why.

It's bad. It's wrong. It's dirty.

It's all the things my mother would forbid if I were still living under her roof. I'm glad that ended a long time ago.

I've never had anything this … arousing happen to me.

It's quite exhilarating, and I tuck the note into my pocket. Then I look around to make sure no one saw me, and I quickly go back inside and shut the door so I can be alone with my little secret.

I open the envelope and take out the note, eagerly reading the typed out words.

She picks up my note and sits down on the edge of her bed, licking her lips.

It compels me to do just that, so I walk to my bedroom and sit down, wetting my lips.

She's so beautiful when she touches her neck, letting her fingers glide down her chest. I wish I could have a taste of her sweet skin.

My fingers instinctively follow the words on the paper, brushing my skin ever so slightly, the tickling sensation arousing.

I watched over her, day and night, saving her from herself as she drinks the nightmares away. I still remember every single second as I peeled away her dress and witnessed her naked body, taking my breath away.

My hand automatically travels to my breast, and I squeeze from excitement. I've never felt this dirty … this sexy over something so wrong.

She was ripe for the plucking as I laid her in bed and watched her drift into a dreamless slumber. Her eyes flutter open, and those dark, rich eyes stare at me for a moment. The realization that she knows hits me. I'm here. I will always be here. Like a silent guardian in the night.

My skin flushes pink from the heat scorching my body as my hand travels down between my legs.

When I left, I needed a cold shower. I ache for her so badly that I can't shake it off. Literally. And now … these notes are the only way I can express myself. Let her know I'm here. Let her know I care. Let her know I want her … so fucking badly.

"I feel it …" I murmur as my fingers dive into my panties. I don't know why I'm touching myself. I just gave in to my body's needs.

Now, she sits on her bed. Touching herself while thinking about me. She fondles her sweet, innocent pussy … because I want her to. She circles her clit and pinches softly, imagining my fingers are toying with her.

Automatically, my fingers play with my clit as instructed. They move by some innate need. Instruments of the dirty composer ... and I'm all too eager to give in.

She feels herself, owns herself. She takes back what belonged to her all along. She's sexy. And she will be mine.

"Yes ..." I moan, my voice heady, intoxicated.

My fingers are inside me, and it's been so long since I last pleasured myself this way. It was forbidden under Greg's command. But I'm no longer his. I'm my own woman now.

I lick my lips and speed up the pace as I let myself go. God, I feel so dirty. So horny. So damn good.

She caresses her nipples, which tighten under her grip, and she imagines my mouth latching onto them, suckling them one by one. But what she doesn't know ... is that I'm watching her through the small gap between her curtains. And as she flicks her clit until it pulses, she climaxes with a moan so loud her neighbor could hear.

The moment I read the words, I come.

I don't even care that I just read that he's watching me. I've gone too far to stop.

A long, drawn-out moan escapes my mouth as I rub myself into bliss. And it feels incredible. Liberating. Until I read the rest of the note.

The man who bought her knows.
He knows where she goes. What she's always dreamed of.
He watches her ... day and night.
He's angry and bitter and wants her to come back.
He knows all the bad things she's been doing behind his back.

He also knows he could never satisfy her needs. She needs a man who will protect her. A man who could give his life.

But he is more important. His wishes are her command. His rule was her life.

To him ... she's nothing but a whore.

I gasp and look away. I don't want to read any more. My high comes crashing down immediately, and I get up and walk to the window, checking to see if anyone's there before I close the curtains and scowl.

I'm confused. Is he trying to make a fool out of me with this note?

Or has Greg secretly been writing these notes and

tricking me all along?

I thought it was my stalker ... and maybe it is ... but what if they're working together now? What if this is all some ploy? Something to get me to trust them, so they can frame me, or make me do something stupid ...

So they can murder me in my sleep.

8

Accompanying Song: "A Reflection" by Trent Reznor & Atticus Ross

Hyun

3.5 months ago

I've been able to hold Greg off for a few weeks now. I've been cooking his favorite meals for him, cleaning the house until it was spick-and-span, even making myself out to be the perfect wife, all while pouring in the drinks until he got drunk so he'd keep his hands off me.

I've been walking around the house in flimsy dresses and sky-high heels to appease him. It fades in comparison to what I had to wear for Max's wicked game that one day during dinner ... or rather, what I *didn't* wear. But still, it feels like I've become nothing more than an accessory.

My husband treats me like just another one of his conquered prizes. Every single day, he finds a reason to tell me this. He also loves it when I dress like a hooker. There's occasional ass smacking, along with pinches and laughs, even when his friends are watching. It's humiliating and degrading, but it's nothing like when he gets in a bad mood, which is something I want to avoid at all cost.

However, today I may have given him a few too many drinks.

He's stammering, going on and on about how I'm such a whore because I had other boyfriends before, even though I only had one, not multiple.

But Greg doesn't believe that.

He never believes a word I say.

God, I wish I'd never told him anything about myself.

"Liar!" he yells as he always does.

And in his wild swinging to get a hold of me, he smashes the glass of whiskey on the ground. It doesn't even faze him.

I try to pick it up, but he tears himself away from the couch and towers above me while screaming, "You fucking bitch. Look what you made me do!"

He smacks me across the face, and I take it.

I take it because I have no choice.

Because calling the cops is useless.

And if I did anything to stop him … he'd kill me.

I touch my face and acknowledge the pain quietly.

"You always ruin everything. You couldn't just save yourself for me. You had to go and fuck all those boys. What did you want with them, huh? You wanted their money too, didn't you? You're a filthy gold digger." He spits on the floor, and some of it lands on my hand.

"You've never even given me one ounce of gratitude. I saved you. I gave you everything you needed. Money. Clothes. A home. A husband. And how do you repay me?" He grabs my chin and forces me to look at him. "You never even kiss me. What kind of wife are you?"

"I am yours …" I whisper. "Please … don't hurt me."

He grimaces and then grabs my arm, twisting it painfully. "You're coming with me." He pulls me up and drags me along with him. We stumble up the stairs, while tears form in my eyes, but he's fixated on only one thing.

The bedroom.

I can see it from the way he looks at me, the primal urges.

He won't wait any longer.

Fear washes over me as he throws me into the master bedroom, slams the door shut, and locks it behind him … trapping us both inside.

With no way out, I close my eyes, letting a final tear roll down my cheeks. Then I block everything out.

Accompanying Song: "Hungry Like The Wolf" by Snow Hill

Now

With a scowl on my face, I look at the sex toys hanging on the racks in front of me. In a split second, I decide to grab three of them—all a different length, two with vibration mode, one with a suction cup—and chuck them all into my cart.

Then I walk off to the cash register, casually throwing in a box of condoms from the shelf and a bottle of lube as well.

The lady behind the counter doesn't even look remotely interested in the fact that I'm buying these things. Not that she should. It's a sex toy shop. But I don't normally come here. In fact, I don't think I've ever been here. I'm just not used to how it's supposed to go.

But it does feel liberating to know I can come in here and buy whatever I want, solely for myself. After yesterday, I really needed to do something for me. Something out of the ordinary, something my parents taught me was wrong.

Screw the rules. Screw the world.

I'm doing this for me.

When the lady's done scanning, she looks up and parts her lips, but nothing comes out. She just stares at my face, and it takes me a few seconds to realize why. I have a big bruise on my face from where I fell on the table while drunk.

She narrows her eyes and mutters, "That'll be forty dollars."

I hand her the cash while she keeps looking up at me, and I try not to notice. I clear my throat as she hands me the bag of toys. "Are you all right?" she asks.

I frown. "Yeah, why?"

"Well, you ... your face ..." She points at her own face now as if it'll support her case. Like I don't know I have a black eye.

"I'm fine," I say, and I take the bag and turn around.

No one needs to know I was being stupid.

No one has to know anything about my life.

That's the wondrous thing about being free. No one who decides what you do. No one makes your choices.

"Are you sure? I can ... help," she says softly.

I keep walking. With a smile on my face, I saunter out the store, knowing full well the lady behind the counter is eyeing my back. It feels nice not to be obligated to tell someone the truth.

When I get home, I park my car and grab my new goodies, eager to try them. However, when I get inside and close the door behind me, placing the bag of dildos on the cabinet beside me, I suck in a breath.

Someone is standing in front of my bookcase, snooping through my books.

He turns around when he hears me.

The book he was holding drops to the floor.

***

Accompanying Song: "Game Of Survival" by Ruelle

DRAKE

She's here.

Like a wolf smells its prey, I sniff and take in a whiff of her perfume ... the scent excites me.

I ignore the book that fell to the floor, as it doesn't interest me right now. My focus lies completely on her. I don't even care that she caught me, that I broke into her home ... All I care is that she's here and that I want her. Now.

I inch closer, and she backs up against the door, clutching the wood as if it's going to help her. As if she wants to leave ... like hell, she wants to. I know she desires me too. I can see it in her eyes that wander all over my body, those lips she licks briefly, and that fucking sexy blush on her cheeks.

She freezes as I step closer, her eyes the only thing moving, skidding up and down my body in a delectable manner. She's so small; I tower over her like a statue. I could wrap my arms around her and then some. I could lift her up and carry her to bed. I could do any of these things ... and she would be unable to stop me.

I lean in and place my hand on the door beside her. My breathing is ragged and heavy; drops of sweat roll down my back. I'm fuming with rage and arousal, and I don't know if I can separate the two. I've hunted her for so long, stalked her in the night, and now that she's right in front of me ... I'm not sure I can control myself.

With my free hand, I brush aside a strand of her black hair, tucking it behind her ear. She sucks in a breath as my fingers softly touch her skin, and the left side of my lips briefly shifts into a smile. Her body tenses as I lower my head and feel the air surrounding us thicken with desire.

Lust has taken over my every waking thought. Ever since she opened up to me so beautifully when I sent her the last note—her playing with herself was a sight to behold—I've been thinking about coming back and claiming what's mine. I knew I needed to have her, and I can no longer stop myself from going after her. Today, I will make her mine.

She tilts her head, looking straight into my eyes as I cock my head and lick my lips, ready to pounce. But then she parts her lips and says, "Wait."

I stop before I kiss her. I was just a second away.

Her hands move up toward my face, but I remain rock hard solid. At first, I think she's going to touch my cheek, but her fingers snake behind my ear, sweetly curling around my short hair before pulling down my hoodie.

I wait as she pauses and looks at me, probably determining if she can let me do what I came here to do. If I'm really here to kiss her … instead of being here to kill her.

Her brows twitch, and for a second, I think I spot a brief smile on her face before she blows out a short breath. Angst fills the room, and the heat between us feels scorching hot. While I trap her between my arms, my lips hover so closely to hers I can almost taste them.

That's when I go in for the kill.

My lips take hers no-holds-barred, and it's the most delicious, most sinful kiss I've ever taken. I know it's wrong—that I shouldn't even be here—but it feels too good to stop.

She doesn't push me away, doesn't fight me, and her lips even open up to mine. I run the tip of my tongue along the top of her lip and coax her to open her mouth, wanting to taste every single inch of her. My cock is already hardening in my pants just from the thought of claiming her body. God, if she lets me, I'll fuck her through the night.

But then she pulls back, sucking in breath after

heady breath, her lips pink and full … so fucking tantalizing.

"You should leave," she murmurs softly, her eyes barely opening to look at me.

"But do you really want me to?" I reply with a low voice, trying to make her see differently.

She bites her lip and hesitates, which gives me the opportunity to lean in and press my lips to hers again. I can't help myself. She's too intoxicating. Too innocent not to taint. I want her so badly, and I don't know why I care so much, but it doesn't fucking matter. I know that I need her and that I won't stop until she's mine.

Except she draws back again, and this time, her eyes are still closed as she whispers, "It's not right. Not now … I'm …"

"You're what?" I murmur against her lips, my tongue quickly darting out to give her a taste of what's to come.

But then those words come out of her mouth … and they make me want to strangle someone.

"I'm still … married."

9

Accompanying Song: "What Have We Done To Each Other" by Trent Reznor & Atticus Ross

Hyun

He wears a frown on his face, and his shoulders slump as his hands come off the door. He looks down at his feet then jerks his head sideways, signaling for me to move.

I slide aside far enough for him to turn away from me and twist the doorknob.

Without saying another word, he opens the door, walks out, and closes it behind him.

I've been holding my breath since I said the word. *Married.*

A chill runs up and down my spine.

I can't believe I told him.

That I said it out loud.

That he was here ... and that he kissed me.

It feels unreal.

I rush to the windows to see if he's there, but he's already gone. How he does it, I don't know, but he's always quick as a bird flying off into the sky, disappearing from view. Just like that.

And the only thing I wonder ... is whether he'll come back again.

I close my eyes and shake my head, telling myself to stop. I can't let myself go like that. Not when ... Greg could be watching.

What if he saw him come inside?

What if he watched us kiss?

What if?

So many questions and I don't even know if any of it is even real. I mean the notes told me he was, but they could be lies. Then again ... why would he lie? What does he gain from all this?

I clutch the curtains in front of the window and sigh. I can still feel the heat of his lips, scorching on mine. Just thinking about it makes my pussy thump. God, he was amazing. I can't believe I let myself go like that. It's as if he did something to me—something intangible but definitely there. I can't explain it. I feel like a totally different woman when I'm around him, and I don't know yet if that's a good or a bad thing.

I close my eyes and take a deep breath. Maybe I shouldn't have told him. Maybe I shouldn't have asked him to leave. It feels bad ... being alone in this house. Especially when I chased away the only person interested in me.

But I also know it was the right thing to do.

I can't have him in my house. Can't let him kiss me. Even though my body wants him so badly.

It's dangerous if we're together. If my husband sees him—if we're seen together—he'll kill us both.

***

Accompanying Song: "Obsession" by Golden State (Animotion Cover)

DRAKE

I sit back and drink my coffee from the plastic cup while watching her from afar. She's sitting only a few seats in front of me, reading a newspaper while enjoying a Frappuccino. Her hair softly waves in the wind, and sometimes, I catch the scent of her perfume.

I turn back to my laptop and write some more.

I can't help myself. When I see her ... smell her ... even taste her ... it makes me want to turn it into words. I'm not great at talking, but I have a way with words on paper that'll wrap any girl around my finger.

But mostly … her.

I'm only interested in her. Not one girl has captured my attention the way she did. Why? Because she needs someone to protect her. To keep her safe and out of harm's way.

Someone who will defend her against enemies … people like her husband.

When she told me she was still married, I was shocked. I thought they'd separated and that she'd filed for divorce, but I never expected her to still be legally bound to him.

Maybe he didn't want to sign the divorce papers. I'd imagine him to be that kind of a dickhead.

My hand instinctively folds into a fist, wishing it could pummel his head into the street and smash it to bits.

However, I need to keep my cool if I hope to stay out of jail.

I need to play this game the way it's meant to be played. Slow and careful.

And right now, my focus lies on her.

She probably thinks I left her home because she told me the truth about her and her husband. That I don't want anything to do with a woman who's still taken.

She's wrong.

I still want her. I still need her, and I will have her … And I don't care what I have to do to make it happen.

Having him in the picture only fires me up that much more.

I lick my lips and focus on the story at hand.

I imagine her getting up and leaving her coffee on the table. She saunters away from the coffee shop, clutching her bag close to her body. I close my laptop and tuck it into my bag, silently following her. She seems unaware that I'm tailing her. But then, as she checks her purse, she briefly glances over her shoulder and sees me. We stare at each other, and time seems to stand still.

Then she goes into an alley, and I go after her. It's a dead end.

I see her looking, trying to find a way out, but there's nowhere to go. She's surrounded by walls ... and me.

I sneak up behind her.

I know it's vicious.

I know it's wrong.

But she did something to me the moment I saw her in the library. With those eyes, she lured me in. They told me she was ready to be taken away. That she was done with the world and needed closure.

I could provide that for her.

She only needs to ask.

Perfect.

Smiling to myself, I close my laptop and stare at her

as she takes gentle sips from her coffee. Then I tuck my laptop away, get up, and go home … so I can print this out and mesmerize her once more.

10

Accompanying Song: "Ritual Spirit" by Massive Attack &
Azekel

Hyun

When I left the coffee shop, I could've sworn he was there.

I saw him.

At least, I think I did.

I don't know why, but it felt like I was being watched. Except when I turned around, no one was there. Still, it didn't sit right, so I quickly finished my coffee and left.

As I get home, I quickly close the door behind me and take a few breaths before settling in. I feel so on edge these days. Nothing feels safe. Nothing relaxes me. At least … not while Greg still lives.

I swallow and turn on the light, which flickers … and then goes out.

Frowning, I turn the switch on and off, but the light remains out. I guess the bulb's broken. So I go to the kitchen and grab a new one then fetch my small ladder so I can change it. I set it down and climb up with the new bulb in my hand. As I twist the bulb off and fit the new one, I notice a small wire hanging loosely from the fixture.

Narrowing my eyes, I pick it up and take it out, stepping down the ladder again. And the moment I turn on the light, I see what it truly is.

A tiny microphone. It looks like a bug.

Who would plant a bug in my house?

My heart is racing as I inspect the microphone, but I know it won't tell me anything about where it came from or who planted it there. However, the only people I can come up with who'd be interested in what I have to say would be Greg … or Max.

But Greg already knows I won't spill the beans … because I can't go to the cops; they're in his pocket. The only one I could talk to would be the newspapers … and it sounds like something Max would be afraid of me doing.

Telling the whole world about their twisted little bride games.

I swallow and think to myself. *Should I call him? Tell him I found it?* No, that would only give him an advantage. I should go to him and let him know I found out about his scheme, and that I'm not playing games anymore. That I'm done with being a part of whatever it is they're doing, and that I want them to stop.

For some crazy reason, this sounds like the best idea to me.

I know it's stupid, going back to that place and falling into the same trap all over again.

However, I know they're really not that interested in me. Otherwise, they would've forced me to stay, and they didn't. They let me go, which means I wasn't what Max and his brothers were looking for.

Good thing because I don't think I could've survived if I was.

I crush the microphone in my hand and tuck it into my pocket. Then I go out and get into my car, driving straight to the place I last knew where Max worked. I hope he's still there.

I park my car not far away from the building, and I go inside.

Trying not to draw any attention to myself, I walk steadfast for the elevator, just as I did the first time I came here when Max invited me. This time, however, I come unannounced.

The man standing near the elevator breaks my stride by saying, "Excuse me, ma'am, can I help you?"

"I have an appointment with Mr. Marino," I lie through gritted teeth.

The man looks me up and down, narrowing his eyes, but then he proceeds toward the elevator and presses the button. "Follow me."

I'm not sure if he believes me, but I don't care, as long as he takes me where I'm supposed to be. So I step inside and wait until the doors close.

The wait feels like it takes forever, and sweat drops trickle down my spine just from being confined in a tiny room with a man I don't know. When the doors finally open again, I breathe out loud and step outside, briefly glancing over my shoulder to find the man still glaring at me.

I ignore it and press on. Maybe he'll call Max and tell him someone's coming to meet him, but I'll take that risk. Maybe he already knows just from hearing me pick up the microphone. But it doesn't matter. I've come too far to turn around now.

So I walk up to his door, knock a couple of times, and turn the handle before he even says I can come in.

He's sitting behind his desk, typing away on a laptop, his eyes only barely reaching above the screen.

"Hyun?" he murmurs, squinting at me.

"Hello, Max," I say, clearing my throat.

He closes his laptop and scoots back his chair, cocking his head. "Well, I certainly didn't expect this. I'm curious why you thought this was a great idea." He smiles. "You do realize how dangerous this is, don't you?"

I nod. "I realize that, but I have to ask you

something and I couldn't do it on the phone."

"Is it about the games?" He raises his brows. "Because that's long over. We don't want you."

"No, it's not about the games."

"I must say … your English has gotten much better since the last time we spoke," he muses.

"Thanks," I say bluntly, not wanting to go into it.

He doesn't need to know I've been taking lessons.

He taps the top of his fingers against each other. "I hope you do realize you're lucky …"

"Lucky?" I frown.

"To be alive."

The air between us thickens.

"And you will be as long as you honor our agreement."

"I haven't told anyone about the games."

He raises his brow. "Not a soul?"

"No one," I say in one breath.

After a few seconds, he says, "Good. Now tell me why you're here."

I fish the broken microphone from my pocket and hold it up for him to see. "Is this yours?"

He frowns, looking at it from afar, and then says, "Where did you get that?"

"So it's yours?" Rage boils up to the surface.

"I didn't say that." His lip quirks up into a smile. "However, if I'm completely honest, it does look like one of ours"—he looks me dead in the eye—"but we aren't tapping you."

"Don't lie to me, please," I hiss. "I deserve more than that."

"*You* left our home. *You* canceled the contract and gave up your spot. As far as I know, *you* don't deserve anything from us."

"After what you put us through? I dare to disagree."

He sighs. "Look, Hyun. I don't understand why you're here. I already told you we're not tapping you."

"Isn't it obvious? Who else would do this? You are the only one who has a reason to do so. You want me to keep quiet about your little game. You're keeping tabs on me."

"Oh, please," he scoffs. "Like we'd need to wiretap you for that." He laughs. "Hyun, I already know you'll never go to the police. Or the media." His face darkens, and the look in his eyes is dead serious like he could kill at any moment. "Because if you did, you know what will happen."

I swallow away the lump in my throat, still trying to remain headstrong, despite the obvious threat to my safety.

"I never said I would," I hiss. "But only if you promise me you won't ever bug my place, watch me, or even remotely contact me in any way."

"I don't even want to, Hyun. You left us, remember? Besides, I already made my choice long ago." He sighs and turns around in his chair, looking out the window as if I'm not even here anymore.

"I don't care. The point is I'm only here to make sure this bug isn't yours."

"It isn't."

"But you said it does look like one of yours." I cross my arms. "Can you please explain?"

"It's possible someone inside the company placed it there without my knowledge. However, the brand that manufactures them is a big one. Many companies use them. I'd say you're at a dead end."

He turns to face me again, this time casually leaning back in his chair, seemingly bored. "Are we done now?"

Maybe he's not lying after all. It sounds more like I'm annoying the crap out of him. Good. It makes up for what he did to me a little bit.

"Hyun, is there anything else I can help you with?" he asks.

"Do you know of anyone who could put this in my house? Someone who'd want to keep tabs on me?"

"No ..." he says, chuckling a little. "Maybe one of my employees after they saw you strutting around the bank. Who knows?"

Like a brick in the face, it suddenly hits me.

My dad works at one of the biggest banking companies. And he said Greg was his boss.

One of the biggest ... is this one. The one I'm standing in right now.

I never thought to ask Greg because I didn't *want* to know. I hate him and my parents.

But now, it all makes sense.

My lip twitches and I search in my purse for my wallet, where I find a small, crumpled picture of my husband tucked away. I take it out and place it on the table in front of him. "Do you know this guy?"

He glances at the picture, only giving it minimal attention. "He looks familiar, but I don't know from where."

"He works here," I say.

"Oh, right!" He snaps his fingers. "I remember now." He taps the picture. "This guy was a friend of my father's. I saw him maybe once or twice. I don't interact with him directly; my VPs do that for me. He's a manager in the finance department."

I sigh and close my eyes. "Thank you."

I didn't even realize a *thank you* had slipped from my mouth. How stupid. I have nothing to thank him for. He's caused all my problems. Because I bet that it's only because of me coming to this bank in the first place, to meet Max, that Greg even remotely became interested in me.

It explains everything.

That he was so slimy when I first bumped into him.

When he came to my parents' house as if he was a regular there.

He already had his sights set on me from the get-go.

"How do you know him?" Max suddenly asks.

"I'm married to him," I mutter under my breath,

snatching the picture away again before Max can grab it. I don't want anyone else to see this. No one can know I was here. If Greg finds out, then ... I don't want to think about what happens then.

I crumple the picture in my fist, which is when I notice Max has been looking at me in a peculiar way. Almost like he actually feels sorry for me.

"You know ... you're free to do whatever you want." He picks up a pen and starts playing with it.

"What do you mean?" I ask.

"Well ... since he's an employee here and all ..."

I frown and cock my head, waiting until he tells me more.

"What I'm saying is, I won't hold you back if you want to do *something* about this ... thing."

Thing. Does he mean my marriage? The bug? Or Greg?

Maybe he means all of them.

But why do I not even remotely feel ashamed for wanting exactly what he proposes?

Because honestly ... I'd love nothing more than to see him rot in hell.

I place my hand on Max's table and say, "I'll do it. But if you want me to keep my mouth shut, then help me ruin him."

One of his eyebrows rises, and a small smile appears on his face. "What do you want me to do? Kill him? Do you honestly think that causing more bodies will help my case? No." He laughs. "I'm not meddling in your affairs. You're on your own."

"You've got to help me. After all those games, it's the least you could do," I plead on his good will.

He purses his lips, thinking about it for a second. "Divorce him. I'll provide a lawyer. Once that's done, I can settle things with him on a personal level."

"He'll never agree to a divorce. I'm sure of it."

"Then I can't help you. I'm sorry. If you'd come to me sooner, before you were married, maybe then I could've given him a different girl, but now that you already married him … I just can't. It's too risky. Too much exposure on my part and I'd like to keep things under the radar on my end."

I take a deep breath and turn around, feeling the tears already stinging my eyes, but I won't let them go free. Not here. Not now. None of these men deserves my tears.

"I'm sorry," he adds.

"Your sorry won't help me when I'm dead," I answer, and I leave without giving him the chance to look me in the eye a final time. Maybe he'll regret his choice once he looks down at me from above at the cemetery where they'll bury my body.

11

Accompanying Song: "Daydream" by Ruelle

Hyun

With a glass of wine in one hand and the crumpled picture of my husband in my other hand, I stare at the fireplace in front of me. It's cozy and warm, but in my heart, it feels like it's freezing cold. The longer I sit here and think about it, the more I want to scream and break stuff.

It's not how I am. How I ever was.

I'm the curious, shy type—the one who's always eager to learn new things. The one who's content with her small life and just wants to make do.

I'm not the girl who wants to go out there and punch people even though that's the only thing I can think about right now. Punching Greg in the face. Twisting his nuts until he screams and begs. Shooting him with my gun.

It scares me. Something's changing inside me, and I'm not sure I'll like the person I'll become if I do any of the things I fantasize about daily. But it feels like I'm already too late to stop it.

With a scowl on my face, I tear apart the picture and throw it into the fire, watching it burn.

I wish I could watch his face burn.

To say I have deep-seated resentment is an understatement. I've never wanted a man to die, but I'll gladly make an exception for Greg. He's the devil himself.

I force myself to remember all the things he's done to me.

Made me out to be a whore, a liar, a bitch, and every other nasty word in the dictionary.

Laughed at my bad English, made fun of my thin physique, my posture. Told me that no man would ever want me and I'd be alone forever.

All those months … he pulled me, hit me … used me in every way possible … dehumanized me.

I'm done. Through with it all.

It's time to turn a new page in my life.

I get up and march to the kitchen, taking a large pair of scissors from the drawer. Then I go to the bathroom where I stand in front of the mirror, grab the bottom part of my hair, and cut it all off. The hair falls to the floor, like a burden finally lifting from my shoulders. The short bob that remains is a stark reminder of what I've been through ... that I'm a survivor instead of a victim, and I choose to open a new chapter.

***

A few days later

"There will be a test next week, so make sure you study hard. Any last-minute questions?" the English teacher asks the class. No one raises his or her hand, so the teacher quickly adds, "Well, have a wonderful day, and I'll see you all next week."

Everyone gets up, and I pack my bags and quickly walk toward him. "I just wanted to say thank you. Your classes have helped me a lot."

"Oh, it's my pleasure, Hyun. Your English is great. You're a fast learner."

"Thank you," I say with a smile. "You're a great teacher."

He smiles and gently places an arm on my shoulder. "Make sure you study hard next week. I'll expect you to ace this test too."

I nod as he winks and leaves the classroom.

I sigh and look down at some of the books I'm still carrying in my arms. I wish I could study even quicker so no one would even notice I'm not speaking my native language. Then again, I have to be grateful for what I've achieved so far. I've come a long way from not being able to speak full sentences. And look at me now, thriving on my own, completely without help.

I'm proud of myself.

With a broad smile, I strut out of class and make my way back home. This time, I didn't drive the car because I really felt like walking out my worries. Besides, it's good for my health. I don't want to become a couch potato even if I'm not safe outside like this. I'll take the risk. It's a safe neighborhood. What could happen?

***

Accompanying Song: "Game Of Survival" by Ruelle

As I traipse down the sidewalk and pass some bushes, something catches me off guard.

Or rather … someone.

Out of nowhere, a person jumps out of the bushes, pushing me so hard I fall down.

A loud bang makes me close my eyes. Another one follows.

The weight on my back makes it feel like something hit me. My ears ring, and my head feels dizzy. The only thing going through my mind right now is whether I'm dead.

A mind-numbing buzz rolls over me as my body is completely covered … the smell of musky cologne entering my nose.

After a few seconds, the weight lifts and I can breathe again. I cough and look up … only to find *him* crawling up from the ground.

The man who watches me … over and over again … sends me secret, provocative notes that make my heart beat in my throat. And now, he's grabbing me, twisting me around in his arms, his hands all over me, his eyes scanning my face.

"Are you okay?" he asks. His thumb softly brushes the sore bruise on my face.

The words barely register, but I manage to nod anyway.

"Where did you …" I mutter.

He licks his lips, his face stern, and his voice darker than before. "I always watch you …"

It doesn't sound like a threat.

And for some reason … it makes me feel warm inside.

He holds out his hand, but I stare at it for a few seconds, wondering if I can trust him. *Why did he jump on me out of nowhere? And what was that sound? Did he try to hurt me?*

When I look into his blue eyes, the only answer I find is his incredible devotion toward me. With just a look, he manages to persuade me to grab his hand.

He lifts me up from the ground and holds me close to his chest, forcing me to smell that same musky scent that exhilarates me. His muscles flex, and I can feel every inch of his skin through the thin dark blue shirt he's wearing underneath the brown jacket.

I look up at his beautiful eyes, which scan the area looking for others, while I feel like I could drown in his. Suddenly, they point at me, and I'm at a loss for words. I can't believe he's actually here … that I'm holding him … and he has his hands on my body.

"Are you hurt?" he asks.

I shake my head. "I don't think so."

A woman on the other side of the street stares at us in shock, her hand on her mouth as she quickly dials something on her phone and starts to call.

"She heard it too …" he murmurs.

A witness.

He grabs my hand and pulls me with him into a deserted alley. "You can't go walking on the street like that, Hyun."

My name … coming from his mouth.

It sounds so sexy …

My mind is going haywire right now.

"You were almost shot," he adds, grasping my full attention, as well as my arms as if to instill fear into me. "You have to be careful."

I nod, my lips parted, but I don't know what to say to that.

I came so close to death. It's unbelievable, and I'm

still in shock.

Someone would shoot me?

Yes … yes, they would.

***

DRAKE

Minutes before

She's safe.

I whisper to myself as I inch closer to his house.

She's in her English class. I saw her enter the building. I followed her there every step of the way.

I look at the watch on my wrist. In ten minutes, the class will be over, and then she'll come walking out again. I still have enough time.

I put on my gloves and go up to the living room window behind the bushes. Hiding as well as I can, I peek through the curtains. When I spot him, my blood begins to boil.

Her husband.

I want to strangle him to death, but doing so would mean implicating myself, and I'm not going to jail. No fucking way.

Instead, I settle for watching him as he yells into his phone.

"Fuck, I hate her," he growls, smoking a cigarette.

I turn my back against the wall and listen through the small gap in the open window as he comes walking toward me and stares out the window for a second. My heart is racing, and I catch myself holding my breath.

When I hear his footsteps disappear, I glance inside again, staying long enough to hear him say, "I wish she was already dead."

Of course, he does, sick bastard. After fucking her over, he doesn't even want her to live without him.

I grab a pen from my pocket and a small notepad, and I scribble down literally *everything* he says.

"What do you want me to do? I'm not fucking divorcing her. *She's mine*, and if I can't have her, no one can! I'd rather die than let her win."

I didn't know he fucking cared so much about her that he'd want her to walk over his corpse before she's free—but I will make it happen if that's what he wants.

"I don't care what you think. Just get it done today!" he spits, and then he throws his phone at the wall.

Get it done today.

If that means what I think it means, I have no time.

She's the perfect victim.

My feet skid on the pavement as I rush to catch up.

She's in danger.

I have to get to her.

Before it's too late.

But what if he gets there before me?

I can't let her die.

I run across the street, barely dodging a truck, which blares the horn loudly as I keep running. There's no time to stop. No time to think. What if he's already there waiting for her to come outside?

Two, three, four blocks.

My heart is pounding in my chest, and my lungs expand to suck in as much air as I can while I keep running, my legs barely able to keep up the pace. But I'm not stopping. Not until I see her strolling on the sidewalk, staring at her cell phone, while a man across the street rummages in his pocket and takes out a gun.

I run as fast as I can across the grass. Through the bushes. Right into her.

***

Now

She's here. She's safe. She's right where she belongs.

In my arms.

I'm touching her.

My hands are on her back ... her arms ... her ass.

And the more I feel her press against me, the more protective—no, possessive—I feel.

Dangerously possessive.

Like I'm addicted to the very thought of her

clutching me.

And the closer she is, the more I want to smash my lips on hers and never let her go.

I can already imagine my hands all over her naked skin, our bodies twisting and turning as we make sweet, fucking love.

But it's so, so fucking wrong.

She's not mine.

She still belongs to *him*.

The man who hates her guts.

The man who doesn't deserve her.

But do I deserve her?

I invaded her space. Rushed over and bumped into her, making her fall to the ground. I gave her that bruise. And now, I'm touching her in places I shouldn't be. Places she didn't ask for. Something she probably can't even think about because I saved her.

But just because I kept her from dying doesn't mean I can put my hands all over her.

I feel bad, so I unlatch her from my body and pull her hands down, making her release me.

"I should go," I say as I look down at her. "Go home. Stay safe. Use your car."

Then I turn around and march off, determined not to let my cock take over my mind.

I should follow the guy who almost shot her instead.

I only briefly saw him, but I know which direction he went.

It's a good excuse to separate myself from her before I do something I can't take back.

Keep walking. Don't look back.

The last thing I hear is her voice, pleading with me. "Wait."

It only makes me walk faster.

12

*Accompanying Song: "Hungry Like The Wolf" by Snow
Hill*

Hyun

Evening

Listening to the television, I sit and drink my tea,
but I don't hear a word of what they're saying. I'm lost
in my mind, repeating the scene of what happened
today over and over in my head.

I almost got shot.

I almost died.

The words don't feel real, but they are.

I keep telling myself I'm still alive. I'm still
breathing, and I'm safely in my home.

Thanks to *him*.

Somehow, someway ... he saved me.

Suddenly, I hear something shuffle underneath my door. I immediately grasp my gun and hold it tight as I sit back and watch the door. For a few seconds, nothing happens. So I get up and look closely. That's when I notice the small piece of paper tucked underneath the door.

I put down my gun and walk toward it. Slowly, I pick it up, making sure to check no one's there, but I don't see any feet in the small gap.

I quickly step away from the door and open the note, reading what's written inside.

I want to know if you're okay.

I can't stop myself. I need to be near you. Especially after I almost lost you.

Did you know your husband wants you dead?

Burn this note.

Drake

This one is handwritten, and it doesn't look like he took much time to write it. Sucking in a breath, I check the back, but there's nothing else on it.

Drake ...

The name alone warms my heart.

An impulse drives me to the cabinet, and I grab a pen and a notebook, tearing out a page to write something down.

I'm okay. For now.
You saved me. I want to thank you.
I know you're here, watching me ... I'm not afraid.

Hyun

I tuck the pen back into the drawer and carefully slip the note underneath the door until it's outside on the steps. Then I wait.

It takes a while, but I hear footsteps, and a shadow appears in the narrow gap. I hold my breath. The note is picked up. The shadow disappears and doesn't return.

I step away and smile.

I don't know why I smile.

It's insane.

I'm insane for even replying.

But it's too late to take it back now. I'm sure he's reading it as we speak.

I turn off the television and throw his note into the fire. Then I sit down at my table and stare at the door while listening to the clock, which produces the only sound in this room. Not long after, a new note slides under my door.

In a frenzy, I immediately reach for it and read.

All you have to do is let me in … tonight.

I swallow and step away from the door, looking at it as if he could magically appear through it. But nothing happens. Not unless I want it to. That's the point of all these notes … permission.

But the thing is I think I already made my mind up long ago.

When I saw him watching … and never told him to stop.

So I smile to myself and hold the note close.

A few hours later, when it's time to go to bed, I open the window in my bedroom wide. Then I turn off the light, lie down on the bed, and close my eyes, waiting until it happens.

But the more I lie here, the more at peace I feel.

The warmth of my blanket envelops me in a cocoon of drowsiness, and soon, I fall asleep.

I don't know how much time passes before a creaking noise makes my eyelids flutter open. In the dark of night, I can barely see … but I can make out a shadowy figure standing in the corner of my room, staring at me.

DRAKE

When I couldn't find the man who tried to shoot her, I went back to my own place. Still, I couldn't stop thinking about her. I had to know if she was safe.

And now I'm here ... again.

In her home. Invading her space.

My breathing is shallow, ragged, as I silently watch her look up at me with those doe-like eyes. She's magnificent, so innocent ... so ripe for the taking.

I don't know if she's ready for me ... but I can't return to where we were before.

Her eyes are skidding across the room, and then they zoom in on me. Her lips part but no sound comes out ... yet.

I place a finger on my lips and shush her softly, a devious smile lingering. I whisper seductively, "Don't make a sound. We don't want the neighbors to hear."

I prowl closer, approaching the foot of her bed without taking my eyes off her. I feel like an animal, raging with hormones that beg me to fuck her. But I have to take it slowly, so I don't scare her.

But as my knees touch her toes, she pulls them back, drawing the blanket back too. I can see her sucking in a breath when I lean over and place my hands on the bed.

She watches my every move as I hover over her legs, my mouth salivating from the mere anticipation of tasting her. Her bare feet are in front of me, and I bend over to kiss the top, my fingers softly sliding up her leg. Her skin erupts into goose bumps.

I bite my lip and kiss her ankle, gazing up at her to see if she's still looking. I want her to see everything I do... everything she makes me do.

Just as I watched her, I want her to be a spectator now.

I place another kiss up higher; my fingers inch up her legs, slowly creeping underneath her blanket and pushing it up as I go. The closer I get, the more her muscles tighten, and it makes me so damn hard.

I suck in a breath as my cock slides along her bed while I kiss her knee. Tonight is not about me, though; it's about her. Tonight, I'll show her how gentle I can be ... how much I could give her if she allows me to be by her side.

Tonight, I'll rein in the beast and control my temper, so she'll learn to trust me.

Every time I kiss her, she freezes and relaxes, and for some reason, it almost feels and looks like it's automatic ... like a heartbeat pumping blood into her veins each time my lips touch her skin.

Still ... she doesn't move.

She doesn't fight back ... doesn't push me away ...
And I see it as an invitation to continue.

The blanket is crumpled up to her thighs now, and she's clutching it close to her chest as if she's too afraid to let go. It's completely understandable, considering I'm a stalker creeping into her home. But there's no reason to be ... I'll teach her not to be afraid to fly.

My fingers slide up her thighs, and she sucks her bottom lip as I reach her panties with my mouth. Looking up at her from underneath my eyelashes, I take the fabric between my teeth and slowly pull it down.

She shudders as my hands slide down along her body while I tug her panties down. My eyes devour her shaven pussy ... and soon, my mouth will too.

When I reach her feet, I pull them off and lower myself on top of her, crawling closer again. She licks her lips and swallows at the sight of me nearing her thighs, and a hampered breath escapes her mouth.

I smile at the thought of how aroused she must be ... and how long she's been waiting for someone to love her the way she should've been loved all along.

With my hands, I gently part her legs and bury my head between, letting my tongue dip out to lick her deliciously wet pussy. Her clit is already engorged, and when I softly lick it, she tenses up.

"Relax," I whisper, pressing a kiss against her skin.

"I won't hurt you."

She's still clutching the blanket as I start licking her pussy, my tongue greedy for her taste. God, I've been waiting forever to finally be able to take her in my mouth and suck her dry. And she tastes like heaven ... so fucking good that my cock pulses in my pants. I harden from just her taste, and I rub myself against her bed as I lick her.

After a while, she releases her pent-up anxiety, and the blanket slips through her fingers. Her eyes slowly close, and she grabs the pillow under her head, her fingers digging in from excitement. I speed up my pace, swiveling around her clit until her breathing sounds heady and intense. Then I insert a finger into her pussy, and her eyes spring open from surprise.

I don't stop.

I circle around and add another finger, still lapping her up as I go.

Her eyes beg me for a release.

So I grant it to her.

"Come," I murmur under my breath, flicking my tongue all over her clit.

She sucks in a few short breaths, her eyes still focused on mine. Her pussy thumps against my tongue and squeezes my fingers, coating them in her sweet wetness. She falls apart, convulsing underneath me, and I take out my fingers and suck them off.

"Delicious," I murmur.

I lean up and push her legs farther apart, zipping

down my pants.

"What are you—?"

I place my finger on her lips. "Shh."

Our gazes lock for a few seconds, neither of us saying a word.

Talking is not my forte.

Fucking is.

My finger lingers on her lips. With gentle encouragement, she parts them, and I slide it into her mouth and whisper, "Suck."

Her mouth forms an O, and she sucks her juices off my finger. And fuck me; I can already imagine her sucking my dick until I come. I want to—so fucking badly—but for now, I'll go easy on her.

"See how good?" I murmur, smiling when she nods.

I take my finger from her mouth and hook them under my shirt, pulling it over my head. Her eyes are glued to my body, and she licks her lips at the sight of my abs. I flex a little bit to see her eyes widen, making me grin.

I position myself between her legs, taking my cock from my boxer shorts. Her eyes hone in on it as if she found something she likes ... and I totally understand, considering the length of my dick.

I grab her hand and hold it near her mouth. "Spit."

She does what I want, without even asking why, and I wonder if she likes it that way. Being told what to do ... when to do it ... exactly the way I like it.

I bring her hand to my cock and slowly massage myself with it, letting go after a few seconds. She continues, and I lean back against my heels and close my eyes, enjoying the feel of her beautiful hands on my naked skin. God, it's been such a fucking long time since someone last touched me like this ... It makes me want to come all over her.

She jerks me off in just the right way, applying pressure at the tip, exactly where it makes me moan out loud.

I have to take her hand off my bouncing dick before I shoot my load. I don't want to come ... yet.

She's still lying down like a pretty doll while I hover above her on my knees. I hold her hand right above my V-line, and I put the tip of my cock against her entrance, slowly pushing in while she holds me. I want her to indicate if I'm going too far ... if I'm going too fast ... but she doesn't stop me. Not even when I'm fully inside her.

My veins pulse with greed, and I pull out and thrust back in again, covering it with her sweet wetness. God, it feels so fucking good that I almost can't constrain myself.

Pushing her knees up, I increase my pace, fucking her while she remains silent, her hand still touching my body. I prefer it this way ... no talking ... just sex. This is how I tell her how much I want her. How far I'd go for her. How good I could be to her.

Talking only complicates things ... and our

situation is already complicated enough.

I bite my lip while thrusting into her, and I slide aside the blanket to look at her perky tits hiding behind the bralette. With a single tug, I manage to pull it away, uncovering her nipples. As I tug on them, she closes her eyes, soft moans escaping her lips.

It turns me on so much that I grunt and latch onto her knees to fuck her harder, and soon, the entire bed begins to creak. I pound into her, giving her everything I have. Her nails dig into my skin, and her muscles tighten again, so I rub her clit once more.

I can feel her explode against my dick, sucking me in further, and it feels so damn good that I come.

Growling, I release my seed inside her pussy, thrusting in multiple times to coat her entirely. I don't want any of it to drip out. I want it to stay inside her, so she remembers who gave her this delicious evening … so she remembers she's mine and no one else's.

With a ragged breath and a spent cock, I finally feel sated, and from the looks of it, so is she. I take a few deep breaths as I pull my cock out and tuck it back into my pants. I grab her hand, bring it up to my mouth, and give her a kiss on the palm.

Then I gently slide off her and zip myself up again.

But when I turn around to make my way toward the window again, she murmurs, "Stay."

I glance over my shoulder and look into her doe-like eyes, which burn a hole into my heart.

"Please," she adds.

I think it over for a few seconds, wondering if what I'm doing is really right.

If I should stay to comfort her or if I should get out of here before someone catches me.

Someone we both know will kill me if he finds me in her bedroom.

But her face is so beautiful, and the more I look at it, the more I drown in her eyes. I can't walk away after that. It doesn't feel right.

So I turn and march back toward her bed. She scoots over to make a place for me, and I slide beside her on top of the blanket. I don't touch her ... all I do is stare at her beauty. I can't help myself. I've fallen so damn hard.

She looks right back at me, and there we lie, in complete silence.

Waiting until one of us falls asleep.

Of course, it isn't me.

My heart is beating way too fast. Especially when she mumbles something incomprehensible and rests her head on my chest as if we're a couple. As if that's an actual possibility.

I smile to myself and close my eyes as I hear her take in short breaths while she sleeps, enjoying the feeling of having her close to me while it lasts.

13

Accompanying Song: "Violent Delights Have Violent Ends" by Ramin Djawadi

Hyun

The next day

My eyes flutter open at the sound of a bird cawing outside. The window's still open, and the sun shines brightly, making me squint. It's such a pretty sight, yet when I notice the silence around me, the serene moment is completely broken.

Turning around, I realize he's gone.

Did I dream everything?

I force myself to remember everything that happened last night. From his entry to the way he slithered onto me to how he kissed me down below …

to him being inside me.

Oh god.

It was so good.

It's been such a long time since someone made love to me that way.

I could feel it in my bones, in every vein of my body … the ecstasy.

Yet he's gone.

Disappeared like a mere sigh left by the wind.

I sit up straight and touch the blanket he rested on. I bring it to my nose and smell. He was definitely here. I can still smell the musky scent of his aftershave, and it makes me feel giddy inside.

So I didn't dream it after all.

I feel so stupid for even thinking all of this. Getting all excited when he just up and left.

I stretch out and yawn, but when I turn around to get out of bed, I notice a piece of paper lying on my table. With furrowed brows, I pick it up and unfold it. My stomach flutters. It's another typed out message from him.

I'm sorry for leaving so abruptly. We can't be seen together if you want to survive.

I know there's still another man.

It's why I can't have you for myself … and I hate it.

But I want you to keep all the notes I send you. It's my way of staying in your life even if you don't want me there … even if I'm not supposed to be there.

So keep them safe.
Maybe it'll make a nice story for a book one day.

I suck in a breath and hold the note close to my chest, wishing I had more of him than this silly little piece of paper. I wonder why he chooses only to pen things down instead of talking to me. Maybe he isn't comfortable talking about this … thing we're doing, whatever it is. And for some reason, I want to reply.

So I open the drawer and take out a pen and a notebook. Tearing out a piece of paper, I start writing.

I wish you'd stayed. Is that such a bad thing to want? Even when it's wrong?
I don't care anymore.
If this is how you want to communicate, then so be it.
Do you want me to write back? Is this how you like it?
I don't care if it's weird … I'll do it if it means you'll come back.
I just wonder why you like to write so much … is it a hobby or a job?
Can't wait to read your answer.

I put the pen down and grab some tape, biting a piece off so I can stick my note to the window. I don't care if it's in full view of everyone else. No one except him comes there anyway, and I know he'll be back to watch me. It's only a matter of time.

I put everything away and quickly put on a pair of sweatpants and a casual white shirt so I can have my morning cup of coffee and walk out to grab my newspaper.

But a sudden ringing phone makes me jolt up in shock. I run to the living room and pick it up.

There's nothing but silence.

"Hello?"

No response.

"Who is this?" I ask, sweat prickling the back of my neck.

A thud and beeping follow.

I pull the phone away from my ear and stare at it for a few seconds.

What the heck?

Frowning, I put it down, grab my laptop, and sit behind my desk. I open a browser and immediately type in the number shown on the caller screen.

The number that appears makes my stomach roil.

It belongs to Greg.

Why did he call?

And why didn't he say anything?

Is he checking up on me? Or is he genuinely stalking me too?

An eerie shiver runs up and down my spine.

I feel on edge.

A loud banging on the front door makes me squeal.

"Hyun? Open the goddamn door!"

My heart practically pounds out of my chest.

It's him. Greg.

He's here.

How does he know where I live? I never gave him my address.

Oh god, what do I do?

"I know you're in there!" He rams the door so hard it almost unhinges.

"I know you're sleeping with someone," he scoffs.

At that moment, it feels like my heart stopped.

How does he know? He couldn't have seen? Unless … Drake is working with him.

"You fucking whore! You think you can fuck around without me noticing?" he screams, still jerking the door handle.

I quickly rush to grab my gun and point it at the door, my hands shaking.

"LET. ME. IN!" His voice booms so hard, it feels like it goes straight through my chest.

I can't breathe … I can't breathe …

He's here … he can't be here …

I have to get away from him.

So I do the only thing I know how. I turn around, go to the back door, drop my gun and run.

3 months before

I place the bowl of lettuce and peas on the table as quietly as I possibly can, trying not to disturb the conversation Greg and his friend Mr. Reed are having. He and his wife are visiting for a business talk and to meet me. Greg was all too happy to show off my butt to Mr. Reed, slapping me in his presence to humiliate me.

I've grown accustomed to it.

My husband laughs and drinks wine while I get to pretend-play the housewife and perfect cook.

However, a chair standing in a place I'm not used to makes me stumble, and I drop a plate filled with potatoes on the floor.

"Fuck!" Greg yells as I shoot down to the floor to pick up the broken pieces of plate.

"Look at what you did!" he screams.

"I'm sorry," I say, looking up at his angry face. I hate apologizing. I hate that he does this to me, but words help me not get hurt … and I will use them to save myself if I must.

"Sorry doesn't unbreak the plate. Sorry doesn't give us the potatoes back!" He kicks one away, exactly the one I was about to pick up.

Suddenly, he grabs my wrist, pulling me up … and

it hurts.

"Ow …"

"You think this is a game?" he spits in my face.

"No …" I hiss. "You're hurting me."

"Greg," Reed says, distracting him momentarily. "It's only potatoes. I don't like them anyway. Let's just let her clean it up and enjoy our dinner."

Greg snorts and grimaces at me. "I'll be lenient— this time. You'd better be grateful."

When he releases me, my blood rushes to my wrist, and I feel the mark he left searing into my skin.

I quickly grab the potatoes that are still on the floor, rush to the kitchen, and dump them in the trash. Before I go back inside, I wipe away the single tear running down my cheek and grab a glass of water, chugging it down in one go. Then I straighten my dress and go back inside.

Everyone looks at me, but I ignore them, and soon, they return to their normal chatter.

When I sit down to eat our meal together, they all raise their glasses and toast to the good food and to a great evening. Greg skips my glass, but I don't care.

I sit in silence and watch them talk, smiling whenever Greg mentions how much he likes my body to try to keep up the appearance that I'm okay with everything he does and says.

Of course, I'm not okay.

The constant bombardment of attacks and swear words get to me. Words like whore, bitch, useless brat, pig, slant-eyed, monkey … you name it, and he's said it straight to my face. And worst of all … the more he uses them, the more I'm starting to believe them too.

I don't want to. No one does. But when you live in an environment like this twenty-four-seven, you're bound to succumb to it. I'm no exception, and it makes me feel weak.

Sulking, I stare at my wine glass and ponder whether I should just kill myself to be free of this. To be free of him.

But then I see *her* staring at me.

The woman Reed brought with him.

Annushka, his wife.

We engage in a stare that neither of us seems to be able to look away from.

There's a reason, and we both know why.

The entire evening, I've seen her avoiding her husband, not talking to him, not even looking at him or acknowledging him. The way she looks and acts, stiffly, out of this world, like she's somewhere else with her mind … I recognize it.

I act the same way when I'm around Greg.

"She's a really good housewife, don't you think?" Greg boasts about me to Mr. Reed. "Nice and quiet. I'm so glad I invested my money in her."

They laugh a little as if it's the most normal thing on earth.

"Well, Annushka isn't so bad either. She's fucking amazing in bed."

Annushka's cheeks redden, and she drowns herself in her wine.

Greg eats his steak like a slob, spilling the juices all over his shirt. "Oh yeah, how much did you pay for her? Can't be much, I mean, she doesn't look like she'd do the dishes and clean your house."

"A lot, and trust me when I say she'll do *anything* I say." Reed folds his arms as if it's something to be proud of.

I almost gag on my veggies, and I swallow them down with some water and then some wine to ease my mental images.

I look at Annushka and give her a faint smile, one that says "I'm here with you; I know what you're going through." I don't know if she gets it. I don't know why I do it. But a brief smile back is all I need to know that I'm not alone. She's not alone. And as long as we realize this isn't normal, and that someday, we're going to escape ... we'll make it.

And at this moment, I decide I'm not going to give up my life that easily.

Greg can take my home. My money. My body. My dignity.

But he'll never take my heart and soul.

Only I can give that away.

14

Accompanying Song: "Logos" by Ludovico Einaudi

Hyun

Now

I park my car far away from the building and grab my cell phone, calling Annushka's number. "Hey, it's me. Are you alone?"

"Yeah. Why?"

"I'm standing in front of your building. Mind if I come up?"

Mr. Reed is a lot less strict than Greg is when it comes to giving Annushka privileges. She can go where she wants, as long as she tells him beforehand, and she can even invite people to the house.

"Uh, sure ... Are you okay?" she asks.

"No, not really," I mutter as I walk in and go to the elevator, pressing the button to her floor. "But I'll be right there."

I turn off the phone and tuck it into my pocket while waiting for the elevator to finally reach the floor she lives on. I know exactly where to go because she told me where she lives. We've been in contact with each other ever since that dinner with the four of us. In secret, of course. We send each other emails and talk on the phone for short amounts of time when our husbands were away. We talk about them and how difficult our lives are. She helped me get through those painful months.

And even now, when I don't know where else to go to feel safe, I go to her.

Even when she's married to another monster.

As I approach her door, I'm about to knock, but she opens it before I do.

She grabs my arms and checks around the corner. "No one followed you?"

"No."

"Good." She bats her fake eyelashes as she stares me down. "Then get in."

She pulls me inside and slams the door shut behind me. "Sorry, I have to be careful," she says as she takes my coat.

"I understand," I reply. Mr. Reed doesn't like unwanted visitors. Only friends he can trust. And I'm not sure which category I belong to now.

She walks to her kitchen and puts on coffee. "Want some coffee?"

"Yes, please," I say.

She chuckles. "You don't have to be so cordial to me, you know. You can say 'yeah.' Or something. I don't know." She shrugs.

"Thanks, I'll remember that," I say, smiling. She smiles back and puts some coffee in the pot.

"Go on. Sit down. There's plenty of space." She points at the couch and the chairs near the fireplace.

I was still admiring her home because it's so damn huge. I've never visited here, but now that I have, I understand why Greg always seemed to want to boast to Mr. Reed about something. It wasn't because he was so proud. It was because he was trying to one-up him.

Greg is jealous of Mr. Reed's wealth.

I smirk as I sit down on a velvety red chair, sinking all the way down, which looks ridiculous. Before Annusha returns with the coffee, I quickly push myself up and try to sit as natural as possible.

"So how are you doing?" she asks as she puts down the cups.

"Thanks," I say, picking up the cup. "Not so good."

She sits down next to me and casually folds her legs on the chair, almost sitting in a cross-legged position. "What happened?"

"Greg ... he was banging on my door, screaming at me." Annushka knows I moved into a new home away from him. I hold the cup close to my chest to let the warmth flow into me. "He found out … I was …"

"What?" She lowers her head.

"Nothing." I shake my head and sigh, trying to wave it off as a silly thought, but she's not falling for it. Damn. I shouldn't have opened my mouth. It sounds insane when I think about it.

"Tell me what he found out, Hyun," she says.

"I can't."

She grabs my hand and squeezes. "You're shaking."

I pull my hand away and look down at the swirling coffee in my cup.

"You know you can talk to me, right?" she says, leaning over to grab a pack of cigarettes off the table. She takes one out and holds it out to me. "Here."

"Oh no, I don't smoke," I say, putting my coffee down.

"Try it." She keeps waving it at me, so I take it. "It'll make you feel better."

She fishes a lighter out of her pocket and raises a brow at me. "C'mon …"

I sigh and put it in my mouth, after which she lights it.

She throws the lighter on the table and says, "Take a drag. It'll feel shitty at first, but then you'll feel a lot better. Trust me."

When I do, the smoke burns my throat, and I cough.

She laughs. "Told you it'll feel shitty. Just take a few

more. You'll be relaxed in no time."

"Is that what you do to cope with Reed?" I ask, putting the cigarette in the ashtray.

Her face turns sour immediately.

"Reed and I don't talk a lot," she replies, toying with a loose strand of her silky white hair. "I like it better that way."

She and I both know much more goes on behind closed doors. Things we don't tell anyone because it's hard to talk about. And if she does want to share … I'm always there for her like she is here for me.

"So tell me why you came here," she says, clearing her throat. "You wanna talk, so let's talk." She places a hand on my leg. "Don't be afraid. I won't bite." She grins.

I smile awkwardly. "Well, I feel like someone's trying to kill me."

She frowns and then bursts out into laughter. "Sorry. It's just that it's nothing new to me."

"Oh." I look away for a second, trying to imagine what it must be like for her living with Mr. Reed. Probably just as bad as it was when I was still with Greg.

"What makes you think someone wants to murder you?" She supports her head with the palm of her hand as she leans against the chair.

"Well, a few days ago, someone shot at me."

"Oh my god. Really?"

"Yeah, and then today, Greg showed up at my door

screaming that I'm a whore."

"Oh, boy." She makes a face.

I smash my lips together. "He was pounding my door so hard I bolted. I couldn't stay there, knowing he could burst in at any moment, so I left through the back door. I only barely made it to my car before Greg came after me. He even jerked the door handle and slammed the windows with his fist. I was terrified." I look at my own shaking hands, wishing for it to stop. "My mind was blank when I hit the gas. I didn't know where else to go. I'm sorry."

"No, don't be sorry." She pulls me in for a hug and pets my back. "Oh, honey … I'm so sorry for you. You did the right thing by coming here."

"I'm putting you in danger. What if Greg finds me here?"

"How's he gonna get inside?" she muses, pushing herself away from me so she can look me in the eye. "Over my dead body." She smiles. "Chin up, girl. You got away from him once; you can do it again."

"Will it ever stop?"

She narrows her eyes. "Only you can make that happen."

I swallow away the lump in my throat and nod.

She grabs the cigarette again and stuffs it in my mouth. "Take a drag. You'll feel better."

I do what she says, and this time, she's right. It does take the edge off things.

"See?" She smiles.

"I feel much better now that I'm here. I always feel so alone in my home."

"Hmmm … even with your lover there?"

My eyes widen. "What did you say?"

"Oh, honey." She grabs her cup of coffee and takes a sip. "You didn't think I didn't know about your secret lover, did you?"

"How—"

"Our husbands talk with each other, you know," she says. "He's all over our floor on a weekly basis, now that you're gone from his life." She rolls her eyes. "I wish he'd crawl back into that stinking hole he came out of. I'd kill him myself if it wasn't for—"

"Your husband. They're friends … and friends tell each other everything," I mumble, still in shock.

"Exactly," she muses.

I suck in a breath and get up from the velvety chair. "I have to go."

Her brows furrow. "Already?"

"I can't." I stumble my way to the door. "I'm sorry. We'll talk later, okay?"

"Hyun," she says, but I don't really listen anymore. "Be careful."

All I hear are the voices in my head, telling me how stupid I've been.

Talking to Annushka. Telling her all my dirty secrets.

Not even realizing that she's married to Greg's best friend, and he probably demands that she tell him everything I tell her. Just like he tells Greg whatever I told her.

Like where I was going to live ... what I'm doing and where I'm going every day ... that I wanted to kill him.

Greg knows everything.

15

Accompanying Song: "Hungry Like The Wolf" by Snow Hill

Hyun

I almost drive through a red light.

That's how agitated I am.

I'm stuck in my head, wondering if I shouldn't have made such a rash decision, leaving her house without even telling her why. Without even saying a proper thank you and goodbye.

I don't like to be that person. But I don't trust anyone anymore, and when I feel threatened, my first instinct is to run.

I hate it, but I have no other choice. Fear makes you do that.

I sigh and wonder if I should call or email her to apologize.

Or maybe I shouldn't talk to her again. It's the safest thing to do for both of us, even if it isn't what either of us wants. At this point, I don't know what the best decision is. Losing a friend or being at risk?

There's no going around it; I'm screwed.

A horn blares in my ears, and a man in a passing car sticks up his middle finger at me.

I almost drove into his lane.

When Greg said I was a bad driver, he was right … even though I hate that part. Some things aren't fixable. You just have to deal with them the best way you can. In this case, it's ignoring whoever gives me the finger.

As I drive my car up to my house, I spot a man sporting a hoodie going into the forest right behind it. Gawking out the window while driving, I almost drive over the curb but manage to hit the brakes on time. I quickly park my car in the driveway and jump out, following him into the woods.

It's Drake—I'm sure of it. I can tell from the clothes he's wearing and the way he walks, with his shoulders slumped, even though he has enough muscles to hold him up. Like he doesn't want to be noticed.

But I noticed him.

From a distance, I stalk behind him, hoping he doesn't spot me. I don't want to be seen. This time, I'm the one who watches.

I follow him all the way into the dark part of the wood, deep and far away from any street. *What is he doing here?*

A twig breaks under my feet.

I inhale and hide behind a tree before he turns around.

Did he see me?

God, I hope not.

I feel like a fool for doing this, but I want to know where he's going and what he's doing. I already have enough on my plate as it is with Greg, and I need to know if I can trust Drake.

After a few seconds, I take a leap of faith and look over my shoulder. He's started walking again, but he's far in the distance, and if I don't follow soon, I'll lose him. So I pick up the pace and use the trees to stay hidden when needed.

It takes a while before I finally see where he is heading.

A cabin sits in the middle of the woods with a small path that looks like a dirt road leading up to it, presumably for a car … if he even has one.

I wait a while before I follow him again. I don't want him to notice me.

Then I look around the premises to see if he's there, but I don't see anyone. And for some reason, it makes me want to go inside.

That's insane.

But I can't stop myself from approaching the house

anyway. Can't stop from slowly turning the doorknob, which slides open with ease. It wasn't locked.

What are you doing? Get out of here, Hyun.

The little voice inside my head is screaming, but I continue anyway.

I want to know what he's doing here.

But as the door pans open, I realize … he lives here.

With the poor lighting, I can barely make out the inside, and I squint to get a closer look. A shoddy couch sits in front of an old TV that still has antennas, and in the corner is a makeshift kitchen with a small fridge and one stove, which is covered in dirty dishes. There's a table somewhere too, but clothes and more dirty dishes covers it. In the corner, right next to the door is a desk filled with stacks and stacks of papers and pens, and buried underneath is a small laptop along with a printer. Above that are countless Post-its hanging from the wall, scribbled with notes. And next to that is a doorway leading to a room with an unmade bed.

The whole place is a mess.

Understatement of the year.

In the left corner, I spot a bookcase filled with books, and the beautiful collection instinctively draws me to it. I don't know why, but I love the scent of ink on paper, and when I see books, I want to touch them and smell them all. Is that weird? It must be.

I grab one of them titled *Kept in the Dark* and flip

through the pages. I bring it up to my nose and take a quick whiff. Nothing wrong with smelling books. At least, that's what I tell myself. I quickly put it back and grab another one called *You Never Saw this Coming* … with the subtitle "How To Write Plot Twists Like No Other." Inside is a bunch of methodical explanations on how to write the perfect novel.

It explains why Drake loves to write so much. I mean with the printer, the laptop, and all the notes he sent me. It makes perfect sense.

Suddenly, the front door slams shut, and I squeal, dropping the book on the floor.

When I turn around, I can barely make out the figure standing in front of me, but I know it's him. I can smell his intoxicating musky cologne and feel his penetrating stare.

I hold my breath as he bends over and picks up the book, holding it out to me as if I'm supposed to take it back. I slam my lips shut and wait. He frowns and then leans past me, hovering so close to me I can practically touch his skin. My heart skips a beat as I close my eyes, feeling the hot air waft past me as his hand reaches for the bookcase and places the book back where it belongs.

For a second there, I almost forgot what he was doing and thought he was going to kiss me on my neck.

Silly me.

But then, as he inches back, I feel his lips brush my

skin.

***

*Accompanying Song: "Obsession" by Golden State
(Animotion Cover)*

DRAKE

She's here. Out of all places to be, she came to my home.

My territory.

Like a butterfly flying straight into the spider's trap.

I can smell her, taste her fear, see it in her eyes, and it makes me want to claim her. Right. Now.

She came into my house, thinking she could snoop on me, but I already knew she was following me from the start. I waited for her to come after me. I'd planned it.

I wanted her to see my life … my home … me, for who I really am.

An obsessed recluse who lives eerily close to her.

It's *not* a coincidence.

I hover near her, and I feel the magnetism between us. I only picked up the book she dropped to use it as an excuse to get close. She's standing perfectly still, like a model waiting to see if she's passed her inspection. I lick my lips, my senses electrifying from almost touching her. Her body is within my reach, and all I need to do is grasp it.

And as the book hits the shelves, I let my lips roam freely over her neck. I can't stop myself anymore. I don't want to.

She came here of her own free will.

That means something ... it means she trusts me enough to want to seek me out.

Maybe she needs someone who will give her undivided attention when no one else does. Something no one else can do quite like me. Something so good ... she just has to have it.

So I kiss her skin and listen to her suck in a breath. I plant my hand against the bookcase and trap her between my arms. My tongue darts out for a few quick, sultry kisses, and I can feel her body inching toward me, her breathing ragged. My dick is already hard from the sounds she makes, and I can tell she's getting hot and bothered too.

But then she clears her throat and pushes me back. "No."

I cock my head and look at her beautiful lips. "No?"

She licks her lips, biting them, not answering the question.

It's as if she doesn't even know what she wants anymore.

I sigh and turn around, casually sauntering toward

the bathroom.

"Where are you going?" she asks.

"Shower," I grumble, annoyed with her indecisiveness.

My cock tents my pants, and I will it down, but it's not happening. So I take them off, along with my boxer shorts, socks, and shoes. Then I pull off my shirt and throw it in the corner of the bathroom on the pile of clothes that was already there.

When I turn around to grab some shampoo, she's still standing in the living room, blatantly staring at my naked body while blinking rapidly, her lips parting ever so slowly.

A smirk grows on my face. "Seen a ghost or something?"

Her face glows red, and she stutters, "I can't believe you just took off your clothes while I'm still here." She swallows, visibly confused. "Do you want me to go? I can go."

I shrug. I don't see the problem. "You can stay." I give her a smile, and she tentatively smiles back, trying to hide the obvious stare. I guess my cock stole the show.

"Okay," she murmurs as I turn around and turn on the shower, wondering if she's staring at my ass. She probably is, judging from the squeaks in her voice. "I'll go sit down over here…"

I don't answer, as it wasn't a question, and I don't see the point in discussing something completely irrelevant. I'm a man of actions, not of words, and I prefer the written word regardless. I could write whole essays about how her beauty captivates me and about all the things I would do to her to make her mine.

But she already knows that.

She's seen my notes.

Touched herself to my dirtiest fantasies.

And now, I'm touching myself to them too.

Under the shower, my cock has done anything to cool down.

All I can think of is claiming her for my own, and it only makes me stroke myself more. I don't even care that she's in the room beside me. I need the release, one way or another, and if she doesn't want it, then I'll have to take care of it myself.

So I imagine her showering with me as I jerk myself off, picturing her naked body. I hiss and bite my lip, completely immersing myself in my own fantasy. The fact she's right next door only makes it that much more exciting. That much more forbidden.

But when I open my eyes for just a second, I spot her standing in the doorway, with her mouth wide open.

16

*Accompanying Song: "Obsession" by Golden State
(Animotion Cover)*

DRAKE

I stop moving my hand, but my cock is still rock hard, and she's looking at me with a mouth-watering expression on her face. She caught me right in the act, yet she doesn't even seem angry. Or upset.

She just seems … frozen in place.

Completely mesmerized by my naked body.

I wonder what she's thinking. If her thoughts just as devious as my thoughts are.

I brush the water off my face and look her straight in the eyes as I say, "Come here."

With my index finger, I beckon her to come closer. It's not a command. It's an invitation. But if she takes it as such, I'll have no problem with it.

I want to test her limits. I want to know what she'd do. If she'll cross the line between infatuation and obsession. I'm already far beyond that, and she knows. That's why she's staring. Yearning with only a look. Questioning whether she's allowed to look at me … maybe even touch me.

She doesn't need to ask.

"You don't just want to look," I say. She doesn't need to say it because I already know.

I cock my head and beckon her with my hand now.

She finally steps forward, one foot in front of the other, across the slippery floor and through the steaming fog.

Her thin, square-shaped body catches my eye, and I can't help but allow my gaze to roam all over her body, taking in every inch. She looks so young, but she's far from innocent now.

When she's near me, I lick my lips and turn toward her with a full-fledged erection, not giving a shit that she can see it. All I care about is that she's almost close enough to touch it. To taste it.

I look down at her as I tower above her and say, "On your knees."

I wait … she does too … and I wonder if she'll back out. If this is one step too far for her.

But she doesn't. She actually goes to her knees right in front of me, her skirt soaking up the water as she hits the floor.

I swallow away the pent-up arousal that just exploded, making my cock bounce up and down from excitement.

Does she trust me enough to let me do anything to her? Or is this all a test to see whose side I'm on? Regardless … I'm not going to let this opportunity slip.

"Closer," I murmur, and her face moves closer to me.

Without asking her if she's okay with it, I start jerking off. Right in front of her. So close to her face, she could dip her tongue out and lick me. I'd fucking love that, and maybe I'll make her do that in a minute. But for now, I want to enjoy the sight in front of me.

I reach for her face, tempted to touch her … and she actually lets me.

Running my finger gently down her cheek, I spoil myself by imprinting the image of her kneeling in front of me into my mind.

"Open your mouth," I say after a while, my cock twitching with delight when she does exactly what I say.

Her lips part so beautifully that I just have to touch them. I let my thumb slide along her lips and down to her chin. Then I bring my cock closer and brush her lips with my tip, coaxing her to let me in.

The closer I get, the more frozen she becomes, but I don't stop. Not unless she tells me to and I haven't heard a single sound from her throat. That won't last for long, though … that I'm sure of. She'll be moaning by the time I get to her soaking wet pussy.

I gently slide my cock onto her tongue, and it feels so fucking sinful. I want to come right there and then, but I have to control myself. I want to enjoy this moment, so I blow out a breath and relax, letting her do the work.

Her tongue swivels across the tip, tickling my senses. I close my eyes and allow her to explore. Her mouth is wet and soft, and I can feel she's getting into it the more time passes because her strokes get faster and she begins to suck.

So I take the opportunity to slide in deeper and tell her to massage my balls. She listens to every single one of my commands. It makes me wonder if I'm dreaming all of this. If so, I sure as hell don't want to wake up.

The more she sucks, the harder I become, and I feel the urge to pump into her. So slowly, I allow myself to let go, softly thrusting in and out of her mouth. And she allows me to, goddammit. This is too good to be true.

Her clothes are getting soaked because the shower is still running, and rivulets of water stream down my abs, dripping onto her face. Water won't be the only thing on her face, though … because I'm so fucking close.

The way she looks at me, with eyes that practically spell out for me to take her …

I have to have it all.

I pull back before I come down her throat, but it's

too late to stop, and I don't want to wait anymore. As I jerk myself off in front of her, I come. I come in her open mouth, covering her with my cum. I groan, and my body quakes from the pent-up sexual tension finally releasing … all over her face.

But the more seed jets out, the more I feel I'm not done yet. And even though her clothes and face are a mixture of water and cum, I pull her up by her chin and kiss her. I don't give a damn. The only thing that matters to me is that she lets me.

Instinct drives me to grab her ass and pull her into the shower with me. I don't even care that she's still fully clothed, and she doesn't seem to mind either, judging from the fact that she's allowing me to pick her up and haul her inside.

I shove her against the wall and yank up her skirt, tearing away her panties, as my dick is ready to claim her. I don't wait one second before thrusting into her already wet pussy. It feels so good that I moan out loud, and it makes her mewl too. Her face is flustered, her eyes half-mast, and her pussy so damn warm and inviting.

The water is pouring down on us, but I don't care, and neither does she. All we do is kiss and fuck hard, drowning out the voices in our heads telling us to stop.

Nothing … and I mean *nothing* … will make me stop wanting her.

I kiss her neck and leave my mark on her skin. I lick her wet body, letting my tongue slide all the way down her chest. And as I impale her on my length, she starts rocking along with me, her pussy clenching with need. I can feel the pressure rise, and I know she's about to come, so I thumb her clit softly. Holding her up with one hand, I circle her clit until the pleasure bursts, and her muscles begin to tighten around my cock.

God, it feels so good.

And that sound she makes. I could listen to it every day.

Her face looks beautiful when she comes undone, and the mere sight of it makes me explode too. I come inside her, jetting my seed deep into her pussy. It's the best fucking feeling ever.

I end with a kiss that's as deep as my need for her to be by my side.

I know she will be mine. It won't be long now.

Greg will be out of the picture soon.

17

Accompanying Song: "Last Stand" by Kwabs

Hyun

The next day

I wake up to the smell of bacon filling my nostrils. I take a deep breath and open my eyes, rubbing away the sleep. Thin strips of sunlight pass through the thick, green curtains, blinding me as I look around the room. Fewer clothes are scattered around the room, and I can hear a washing machine running somewhere in another room.

When I throw the blanket off and let my feet sink to the beige carpet floor, that's when it hits me. I'm not in my home.

I slept at Drake's home. Did I fall asleep in his arms?

I don't even remember falling asleep. All I remember is him carrying me to his bed after drying me off completely. I admit I was a bit hypnotized by the way he'd touched me ... and used me for his own pleasure.

God, it was *so* sexy.

What have I been missing all this time? A lot, it seems.

This man knows how to please me. He knows exactly which buttons to push and how to make me do anything he says. It's dangerous ... and intoxicating. All I could think was that I was in his home, and he was in the shower ... and I wanted to be with him. So I did.

Rubbing my forehead, I take a few more deep breaths to come to terms with what I did. It doesn't take me long. For some reason, I feel like this wasn't as bad as I want to make myself believe. For my own sanity, I need to trust him when he says he wants to protect me and not think of all the possible things that can go wrong. Like Greg finding out about this place.

Oh, god ... Greg was at my house ... He already knows I had sex with Drake ... What else does he know?

Shivering, I decide I'm not going to wait and find out.

So I grab whatever I can find of my clothes, which are barely dry at the moment, and put them on. Peeking around the corner, I don't see him anywhere, and I try my best to sneak out unseen.

However, the moment I pass the kitchen, I'm screwed.

"Good morning." His voice is unusually chipper.

Fazed, I stare for a moment ... His half-naked body looks so appetizing I'm salivating. Or maybe it's the bacon he's cooking along with some eggs.

"Okay." He frowns in confusion.

"Uh ... morning," I reply, clearing my throat, trying not to look like I was just about to skip.

"Hungry?" he asks, flipping the egg and bacon on a plate and continuing to the next. He points at the chair at a small round table, which is suddenly sparkling clean and says, "Sit."

His voice alone gets me to sit down exactly where he pointed. I don't know why. He has that effect on me ... like an overpowering need to please him rushes over me. Because he gives me so much attention, I don't want to leave. It's like a drug. I need more.

He puts the plate down in front of me. I smile and say, "Thank you."

He smiles back, not replying, but I know he still thinks 'you're welcome.' Drake isn't a man of many words, I've noticed. Or at least, not the spoken ones. And that's nice for a change. A man who doesn't yell at me but prefers to write things down and speak only when necessary. When it's wanted. It makes every single word precious.

I look around the small cabin and notice it's a lot cleaner. The piles of paper have been stashed aside on a neat stack, the dirty clothes are picked up, and the dusty shelves look shinier.

Did he actually clean because of me? Or does he do it randomly when he feels there's enough dirt lying around?

"Eat," he says, as he practically throws down another plate opposite me and sits down himself.

Awkwardly smiling, I pick up the fork and cut off a piece of bacon, putting it in my mouth. He can't seem to take his eyes off me as I chew, and I feel kind of watched when I swallow.

"And?" he asks.

It takes me a while to understand what he wants from me.

"Oh, it's good," I say, nodding. "Really good. Thank you."

"Good," he replies, eating too.

In silence, we eat our breakfast; the air between us thick with unanswered questions and unspoken words. I feel like he already knows why I'm here. That I was on the run, desperate for someone to hold me close. Someone to give me love, which is something I haven't felt in a long time. And he gave that to me, even though I gave him nothing in return.

I keep running, keep questioning everyone and everything around me, and it doesn't even matter to him. It's like his default position is always to forgive me. And it humbles me.

I sigh and swallow my eggs. Neither of us dares to talk. Maybe it's because we already know there's no need for explanations. Still, we can't go on like this forever. And I wonder who will open their mouth first.

Surprisingly, we're both finished before I finally gather the courage.

"I'm sorry for—"

"Sneaking out?" he finishes my sentence.

I'm flabbergasted for a moment before the redness on my cheeks appears. "How did you—"

"I saw you trying to slip past me."

I put my fork down, not daring to look at him. "Sorry." I feel so shitty, trying to run away when he's only been nice to me. I just don't know what to do about this situation, and it freaks me out. "I just—"

"I know," he interjects. "You don't have to explain."

I nod, still feeling guilty.

"And I agree with your decision," he says.

"What?" I frown.

He picks up the empty plates and brings them to the kitchen. "I think you should go." The way he says it, with the nicest voice ever, makes it sound like he doesn't really want it either yet knows it's the only option. He stops washing the dishes and looks me in the eye. "I'm a stalker. Not a lover."

I sigh and look down at the empty table, wishing I could turn back time, so we're still kissing each other in the shower instead of having this uncomfortable talk.

"Your husba—"

"Don't say it," I say. "He doesn't matter to me anymore."

"I know," he says. "But you matter to him."

"Not in a way that's healthy."

"Exactly." He dries his hands and walks into his bedroom like it's the end of the conversation.

"I don't agree," I mutter.

He steps back into view, waiting for me to finish my sentence.

"With the stalker and lover part," I add. "I've never been loved the way you did me last night." My cheeks glow again, thinking about it.

"I'm glad you feel that way," he muses, and then he turns around again.

I quickly get up and look around the corner, holding the doorjamb, wondering what he's doing, but he's just searching through his cabinets. "If I leave ... will you keep writing me notes?"

He pauses, his body tensing. His lips part, but no sound comes out. Instead, he fishes a cell phone from his cabinet and holds it out to me.

"Keep this."

He stuffs it into my hand like it's mine.

"Why?"

"It's safe." He smiles and then turns around again, searching through his clothes for a shirt.

I clear my throat, trying to capture his attention, but he seems agitated. "You mean it's an untraceable one?"

He nods and takes out a big sweater and throws it at me. "Put this on."

I feel swallowed whole by the fabric, it's so large. "Okay ..." Reluctantly, I pull it over my head, but it comes all the way down my legs like some sort of complete dress ... except, it's a sweater. *His* sweater.

"It'll keep you warm on the way home."

"Thanks," I say. It still has his smell, and it makes me feel all warm and fuzzy. "What do I do with the phone?"

He puts on a casual white shirt and walks toward me, cupping my hands together with the phone tucked safely inside. "If your husband bothers you, call me."

I nod gently, not wanting to disagree, even though I feel that'll only make it more dangerous. If Greg sees him, he might ... no, I don't want to think about it.

But what if they're really in it together? What if this is all a farce, and the cell phone is a trap?

I can't think like that. I have to believe in the good in people. Otherwise, my life will never get better. Even though the circumstances surrounding the way we met are anything but normal. I have to trust my own judgment, and he doesn't feel like a threat anymore.

"This place ..." I mumble, wondering if there's a reason for all of this. "Have you lived here long?"

"No," he replies, not even looking away as he says it. "Only since you came to live here."

I swallow, feeling the warmth flow through my body again, electrifying my skin as the corners of his mouth go up.

"But I like it here ... nice and quiet."

"Not a lot of people," I muse.

"Exactly."

"I get that. I'm the same." I smile. "I like my privacy."

"Privacy … feels good. People don't." He looks away. "But I don't wanna talk about it."

His eyes shimmer, and I feel as though we're connecting on some weird level.

So I grab his arm and say, "Hey, you can talk to me about it. I'm not just here for sex." Shame brings the red cheeks back, but I ignore them this time. "I came here because, even though you're stalking me, I feel like you're the only one I can trust right now." I chuckle. "My point is you can trust me too."

I lower my head to be able to look into his eyes. They seem distant. As if he remembers something he'd rather forget.

He blinks slowly as he looks deeply into my eyes and says, "Been hurt too many times."

18

Accompanying Song: "What Have We Done To Each Other" by Trent Reznor & Atticus Ross

DRAKE

2 years before

Writing has always been my number one passion. Stories filled my head from the day I was born. It was all I ever loved, all I ever could. From the day I picked up a pen, I began penning them down. The words flowed from my pen like a never-ending fountain. I could write for days.

Except … only a select few can write books as a means to make a living, and I was not one of them. No matter how many times I wrote a book and submitted it, no one took the bait. And I realized I couldn't go on waiting for someone to come along and finally pick me up.

Writing, for me, could never be a job.

And I needed a job.

Many writers become journalists or bloggers or even content writers for big companies. Not me, though. If I wasn't able to make money with my stories, I would make money from teaching, my other love. The only thing I could think of to do for the rest of my life that I didn't hate. Teaching was the only great substitute for being a real writer.

So that's what I did after I got out of college ... I teach.

More specifically, I teach others how to write.

Creative writing is my forte, and I love standing in front of the class and helping others realize their passion, even if I know it most likely leads nowhere. I'm the first to admit nothing is worse than lost hope. So I give these people hope. Hope that their stories may one day be read, just like mine.

Most of the students like my classes and almost all of them have good grades.

Except for Anna.

Anna ... the girl who only took my class because she needed the extra credit. She spins everyone around her finger, including me.

At times, we sat together after class and went over her homework in private. I normally never did such a thing, but I could tell she needed it. There was something more about this girl; something deeper than that superficial layer of a vixen she wanted everyone to see. Something she kept hidden. And the more time I spent with her, the more I wanted to dive in and find out what it was. That thing … that made her tick.

And so we spent more and more time together until the lines between teacher and student began to blur. It wasn't long before she kissed me. Before we ended up naked in her room.

I wanted to discover all her deepest, darkest secrets … things no one else knew.

It felt like a story waiting to be read.

But I didn't find anything I could enjoy.

Like all of her victims, I ended up being used.

Used to score easy credit points.

Because after a fight, she told me straight to my face that she was only fucking me to get better grades so she could pass. And when I didn't give them to her, she ratted me out as a pervert.

Now, I'm here, listening as the school's senior administrator scolds me for having inappropriate relations with a student while I'm packing the stuff on my desk and putting it all in a neat little square box. Just like my mistakes.

But not even her betrayal hurts me as much as hearing these words …

"You can never teach again."

Because what use will I be if I cannot write or teach? The only two things in this world that I love. The only things I want to do in life.

I will become useless.

A vapid memory of the man I once dreamed of being.

***

Accompanying Song: "Last Stand" by Kwabs

Hyun

Now

In shock, I stare at him. I don't know what to say. It sounds horrible. All he wanted was for someone to listen, to read his stories. To be someone. His student used his weakness and turned it against him. Betrayed him in the worst possible way, all for her own gain. And when he was down … nothing was left of him because they kicked him out.

"You … a teacher?" I frown, finding it so hard to believe.

He nods, still a little lost in his own memories, judging by the look on his face. "I needed money. Writing doesn't earn money," he mumbles. "At least not books."

"You don't know that. Maybe a book you write one

day …" I say, licking my lips. I don't really know what to say.

"I do. I've tried, trust me."

I pull him close and hug him tight. His muscles feel hard against my soft flesh, but soon, he relaxes and lets out a sigh, hugging me back.

"I'm sorry," I say. "I didn't know that."

"I don't like to talk about it," he replies.

"You don't have to. I get it." I pat his back, and I can feel him lean into me even more.

I can tell he's yearning for attention. Maybe that's why he's been around me so much. He craves being close to someone he could trust. Someone who wouldn't judge him; someone who's been in the same position as he has. Someone like me.

He leans back and cocks his head. "You should go."

"But you …"

"I'll be okay," he says. "I don't want you to get in trouble with your man."

I cringe at the sound of those words coming from his mouth.

"He's *not* my man," I retort. "And he will never be."

"But he thinks he is," Drake replies, raising his brows. "And I won't have him kill you."

Kill. The word alone sends shivers up and down my spine.

He places his hands on my shoulder and lowers his

head. "You're safer if he knows you're not with me. At home. I can keep watch over you."

I nod slowly, still not coming to terms with the fact that I have to leave and that I may not see him again. Because who knows if he's telling the truth. For all I know, he could be gone by the evening. Packed his bags and left this place as if he was never here in the first place.

Stop thinking like that, Hyun.

"Right." I turn and start walking toward his door. Right before I open it, I ask, "Will I see you again?"

His lips quirk up into a smile. "Be safe, Hyun."

Of course, he doesn't answer. Just what a stalker would say.

I roll my eyes and smile to myself as I leave the cabin and go back home.

19

Accompanying Song: "Papi Pacify" by FKA Twigs

Hyun

Of course, he wouldn't let me go without making sure I was safe.

He followed me all the way back to my house, and I pretended I didn't notice him for his sake. He likes it when he doesn't feel caught in the act. I don't mind. It makes me feel much safer as I go back to my home because if Greg is still there, I'm sure Drake will protect me from him. At least, that's what I tell myself because it's the only way I can reason with myself. The only way I can believe Drake when he says he wants me.

As I reach my home, I take a deep breath and look

around the corner to see if his car is there, but I don't see anything unusual. My neighbor is outside in her yard again, sunbathing with a fresh drink, and when she sees me tiptoe around the corner of my own house, she speaks up.

"Hyun? Is that you?"

I stop in my tracks and make a funny face. "Uh ... yeah. Hi! How are you?"

"I'm great, thanks. Is everything okay?" There's a concerned look on her face, and she hisses, "You look scared. If you need me to help or call the cops, let me know."

I guess she knows more than I think.

"I don't know ..." I whisper back. "Have you seen Greg anywhere near my house?"

"Today? Not that I can think of," Lorelei says.

"When did you last see him?" I ask, still clutching the wall of my house like it'll protect me or something.

"Yesterday. I heard a lot of noise, and when I went to check, you were gone, but he was still banging on your door. I saw you leave through the back door."

"Oh ..." I look down, trying to hide my shame.

"It's all right, honey. You do whatever you have to to escape getting hurt," Lorelei says, smiling. "Although, I do think you should get a restraining order if it gets too dangerous."

"I know," I reply. "Thanks." But I feel queasy thinking about it. "So you're sure no one's inside?"

"Yup. I've been baking here the entire day.

Watched the neighborhood like a hawk." She grins and pulls aside the straps of her bikini. "Look how tan I am!" And just like that, this conversation lost any and all depth.

"Wonderful," I reply, giving her a forced smile. "Enjoy your day!"

"You too, honey!" she says as I turn around and quickly walk to my house.

There doesn't seem to be any sign of damage to my front door from a forced entry, so maybe Greg did give up. I breathe a sigh of relief and go inside, locking the door behind me. I hope it was a one-time thing only. Hope. That's a big thing in my life right now because I know it's probably in vain. Still, I won't give up.

The first thing I do when I come home is clean up the mess I made and start some laundry. I want to get back into the rhythm and do all my chores until I can pretend it never happened. So I clean and I cook to forget about Greg, thinking only about Drake and how much he'd probably love this tomato soup I'm preparing.

I wonder if he's spying on me now. Looking right through the window, watching me like a hawk. I fantasize about him jerking off right in front of me, and me enjoying the view. It's so forbidden, so wrong, but it turns me on like nothing else ever has. It calms my soul, makes me feel okay when everything around me is falling apart. When my life is ruined, this thing I have with Drake is all that's left.

So I smile and take a sip of the soup, imagining I'm serving it to him tonight.

Of course, I'm eating alone at a table for one, but I can still fake it.

Besides, when I finish eating, I already know what I'm going to do.

Grab my cell phone and contact him.

I already checked the phone when I got home, and it turns out he put his own number in there. Perfect. With a smile on my face, I start texting him.

Hyun: Hey. Are you watching me?

It takes him a while to reply.

Drake: No. Are you in danger?
Hyun: No. I just wanted to know if you were there.
Drake: I'm not. And if I were, you wouldn't know. Telling spoils the fun.

I grin from his comment, wondering if he's lying just to make me question myself. It only makes me want to go check all the windows and peek outside.

Hyun: I've seen you looking plenty of times before. It wouldn't be the first time I caught you in the act.

Drake: Only because I wanted you to see me.

Hyun: And now, I want you to see me. Did you know I'm not even wearing panties today?

Drake: You don't want to go down this route.

Hyun: Yes, I do.

I lick my lips and get up to look at myself in the mirror so I can give him a more accurate description.

Hyun: I'm wearing a short, red top with a lace bra underneath. And below that a secretary's skirt with black tights. Interested yet?

Drake: Why are you doing this?

A frown appears on my face. He really isn't easy.

Hyun: Because I'm bored.

Drake: Then get busy.

Hyun: I'd rather get busy with you …

I bite my lip to hide a devious grin. I hope he finally gets the message. I want him to come over. And yes, I know how insane that sounds, but I don't care anymore. I'm lonely in this house, and all I can think about is him and what he can do to my body. I'm completely lost to him.

Drake: There's no going back if you do this, Hyun. I don't take sex with you lightly.

I think about it for a second, wondering if this is really the right thing to do. It isn't, but screw what's right and wrong. I don't care anymore. I want what I want.

Hyun: I don't want you to take it lightly. I want this to be heavy. And hard.

I'm already drooling at the thought of seeing his cock again. This so isn't me. But Drake does something to me, and I can't deny it any longer.

Drake: Really? Prove it. Sit down on your bed and take a picture of your pussy. Send it to me.

Hyun: Why?

Drake: If you ask questions, this conversation ends now.

I sigh as I go into my bedroom, sit down on the bed, and take a picture. My finger lingers over the send button, and it takes me a minute to actually gather the courage to press it. But he's already seen me. What harm could it be?

Drake: Good. Stay put. I will be there in a minute, and I'll fuck that pretty pussy raw after I've eaten it.

My heart practically beats out of my chest as I read that. He's so straightforward when it comes to his words that it scares me sometimes. But in a good way.

I put the cell phone away and sit on my bed. Smiling like an idiot, I count down the minutes shown on the clock hanging in the living room. I can honestly say, yes ... I am waiting for my stalker to come and take me. And at this point, I don't care anymore what anyone thinks of that.

As soon as someone rings my doorbell, I jump up and run to the door, patting down my skirt, so it still looks mildly appropriate in case someone passes by on the street and looks inside.

However, when I open the door, the biggest shock of my life meets me.

***

Accompanying Song: "A Reflection" by Trent Reznor &
Atticus Ross

"Hello, Hyun. Wishing I were someone else?"

Greg's raging face is the first thing I see, and it makes me scream.

He latches onto the door as I try to block him out, ramming the door against his fingers several times. He yells out loud.

"You fucking whore!" he hisses. "I know you've been cheating. That bitch Annushka was right."

Oh god, I knew it. He's been getting his info from Mr. Reed.

I told Annushka everything—where I live, how I'm doing, who else is in my life—and now, *he* knows it too.

"It's too late to deny it," he growls, trying to force his way inside.

"Get out of my house!" I yell back, but his foot is stuck in the door.

I look around to see if I can grasp anything in my reach, but the nearest scissors are too far away. I can't go anywhere without giving him free rein of my home. I can't reach for my gun, and I can't win this by force.

So I do the only thing I can do. I scream as loud as I can. Harder than I ever have before. So loud, my lungs feel like they're about to burst.

And for some reason, this sudden outburst of energy that I've been keeping locked inside has him frozen. Completely still, like time itself has stopped, and he's just staring at me.

Then his eyes shift toward something else. To the right ... away from my home.

His fingers unfurl from the doorjamb, and he slowly backs away from my home. With tears in my eyes and sweat rolling down my back, I watch him leave. I'm determined to find out where he's going, so I'll know for a fact he won't come back.

Only when I look outside do I realize what made him leave.

My neighbor. Multiple neighbors, actually. All of them standing outside their doors with their arms folded and with fire in their eyes. They've heard my screaming and yelling. Seen him try to force his way inside. Finally, they know.

With them as my witnesses, Greg has no choice but to consider this a defeat. For now.

However, from the look in his eyes, I can tell ... he's not going to give up. Not until one of two things happens.

Either I come back to him. Or I die.

Part III
The Descend

20

Accompanying Song: "Logos" by Ludovico Einaudi

Hyun

One month before

As Greg eats his breakfast like a pig, I muster up all the courage I've been gathering over the past few weeks and walk up to him, planting the paper right underneath his nose. I've been planning this for so long. Annushka helped me make the arrangements. After all the things he said and did, I'm not staying one more day. Not for my parents. Not for the money. And not for the people working at the coffee shop. I refuse to sacrifice myself for others any longer.

For months, I swallowed all the shit he threw at me. I took it all, thinking I was too weak to stand up for myself. But one thing changed that.

When he tried to give me to one of his co-workers, and I had to lock myself in the bedroom until the man was gone. I can deal with a lot, but I will not let any man trample on my dignity like that. The line has been crossed.

Fear only lasts for a limited amount of time, and even though it prevented me from trying to escape before now, its chokehold on my throat has weakened with every passing day. And now, I've had enough.

I finally made the decision to pull the plug and decide my own fate. To stand up against my fears and face them. I've been waiting for this moment for so long, and now, it's finally here.

"What is this?" Greg grumbles, still chewing on his bacon.

"Divorce papers."

He laughs out loud. "That's a joke, right?"

When he looks up, my face is cold, and his turns from ridicule into sour nothingness.

"You ignorant little brat!" he hisses, scrunching the paper with his hands. "How dare you?"

"I don't want this; I never wanted this, and you know that," I say, trying to remain strong.

"I don't care what you want. You are mine." He grabs my wrist, twisting it. "You don't get to decide when this is over. I do."

"Let go." I jerk my arm away, but a red mark still lingers. I tell myself to stay strong and fight for my rights. "I'm not taking no for an answer."

He laughs again. "What? You think this will actually work? Like I'd actually let you divorce me? I *own* you," he growls. "And last I checked, your parents received my money in exchange for you. You don't want them to lose all that cash, do you?"

"I don't care," I reply, grabbing a pen from my pocket and placing it down on the table beside the crumpled paper. "Sign it."

"You'll lose their respect. They'll never talk to you again. And I *will* ruin you, your family, and your fucking jobs. You'll never have anything in your entire life!"

I try to let my face remain as blank as I can even though I'm boiling on the inside. "It doesn't matter what you say. Nothing can sway me. I've already made my decision."

"And what then? Where will you go, huh?"

"I'm leaving. Where I end up is none of your business," I reply. "Goodbye, Greg."

I turn around and start walking, heading straight for the door that I know is open. It's always been open. I just never dared to make the step. To finally choose me over everyone else.

He chuckles like a madman. "You can't do that. You can't do this to *me*!"

"Watch me," I say, grabbing my bags I so neatly hid underneath a stack of clean clothes.

"If you walk out of here, you'll never be safe."

"You can threaten me all you want, Greg. I know

189

what you can do, and still, I don't care."

"I'll kill you!" he yells, marching after me.

I quickly open the door and run out before he has a chance to catch up, slamming the door right in his face.

I don't think twice before crossing the street and running straight to the nearest bus stop. I timed it right because of the bus right there, almost ready to go. I get in with the ticket Annushka bought for me and tell the driver to hurry because I'm escaping my husband.

And right before the monster can get to me, the bus drives off, leaving a cursing Greg in the middle of the street.

I smile. It's the first time in ages I can finally say I feel good about myself.

Now, only time will tell what the future holds. But one thing's for certain … I will never let a man have reign over my life like that ever again. And if someone even dares … I'll give him hell.

***

Accompanying Song: "Burning Desire" by Lana Del Rey

Now

When Drake gets here, and I let him into my house, I hug him tight, refusing to let go.

"What's the matter?" he asks.

"I just wanted a hug," I say, not wanting to make him worry by telling him the truth.

But he pushes me off him and gazes at me with a stern look on his face. "Tell me the truth."

A pang of guilt stings me, and I swallow away the lump in my throat. "Greg was here."

His eyes immediately flare up, and he barges farther into my home. "Is he still here?"

"No, he left after I screamed. The whole neighborhood heard."

"Good," he says, turning back around to face me. "Did he hurt you?"

I shake my head.

He grabs my arms and lowers his head. "Are you sure?"

"Positive. But I can't say I'm the same."

"What do you mean?" he asks.

"I feel ... different." I lick my lips. "As a person. Since I left him. Since you started following me."

"Different how?" He frowns.

"Different good. Like I can finally say no to him. Like if he'd dare to come inside my house or harm me in any way, I'd shoot him." A tiny smile creeps onto my face, thinking about it.

"That's a good thing. It means he can't control you anymore."

I nod and let him pull me close again. I bury my face in his chest and take in his familiar smell, the scent calming me down immediately.

Still, I can't shake the image of Greg yelling at me, the looming threat of his violence, his voice, and all the memories I have of him. I want it all to disappear, and I realize there's only one way to do that.

Palming Drake's chest, I say, "I want you to replace him."

"How?"

"I can't get what he did to me out of my head. The pain. The yelling. The sex ..." I look away, not wanting him to see the shame in my eyes when I think about what he's done to me.

Drake gently cups my chin and makes me look at him. "What did he do to you? Tell me."

"When I still lived with him, he ... tied me up ... forced himself onto me ... came in my mouth." I still feel icky when I think about it.

"Do you want me to override your memories?"

I nod.

"It will be harsh and degrading. Are you sure?"

I close my eyes, take a deep breath, and say, "Yes. I don't want him there anymore. I want you."

He grabs my hand, brings my fingers to his lips, and kisses them softly. "All right."

Suddenly, he lifts me into his arms and carries me into my bedroom. The look on his face has changed from sweet to stern, and it makes goose bumps scatter on my skin. He places me on the bed and pulls his belt from his pants. Pinning my wrists down, he ties them above my head and tightens them until it becomes slightly painful.

His hand travels down my blouse, and when he reaches between my breasts, he rips it open, buttons flying everywhere. He grabs my breast and squeezes hard, making me hiss.

As I part my lips, he places a finger on my mouth and says, "No talking. You talk, you get punished."

"But—"

He smacks my breast, making me squeal.

"I told you it was going to be harsh. Degrading. This is what you wanted. What *you* asked for. Now lie still and let me use you."

His words sound unreal. Like they're coming from someone else entirely. Like he's changed with the snap of a finger, and it scares me a little.

Is this what I asked for?

Yes … yes, I did.

I want him to replace the memories I have of Greg, even if it means feeling the pain all over again. I'll face it, for myself.

He zips down my pants, unbuttons them, and tears them off in one go, throwing them in the corner. He doesn't even bother with my panties, though. He just rips them off, and I suck in a breath from the sharp pull.

He immediately swipes his finger up and down my slit, not waiting one second before ravaging me. With his other hand, he toys with my nipple, taking it between his finger and thumb and tugging hard. Hard enough to make me squeal again.

This makes him smack my breast once more. Tears sting my eyes.

"Focus on me, Hyun," he growls. "Only me."

I nod swiftly as he keeps rubbing my pussy, owning it completely.

"I'm gonna fuck you raw, and then I'm gonna come in your mouth," he murmurs.

He takes off his own jeans and boxer shorts and pulls his shirt over his head then crawls on top. Naked and buff, he sits between my legs, showing me his rock-hard dick before swiping it along my pussy.

"Who does this belong to?" he growls.

"You," I reply.

He twists both my nipples with his fingers, making me scream. "I didn't hear you."

"You!" I yell.

"Good. Because I'm gonna take what's mine now."

Out of nowhere, he shoves two fingers up my pussy, making me clench and suck in air like nothing else.

"Deep breaths, Hyun," he says, swirling around inside me. "I'm not done with you yet. Not for a long time."

After he thrusts a few times, he pulls out his fingers and licks them. "Delicious." Then he leans up, grabs my body, and twists me around, so I'm on my belly.

"What are you doing?"

He smacks my ass so hard I jolt up and down.

"I said no talking!"

My lip quivers as he rubs my other cheek, wondering if he's going to smack that too. This feeling of anticipation is all too familiar, but the last time it was done wasn't in trust. Now it is. I trust him.

I trust him. I trust him.

This mantra helps me turn this experience into something positive, allows me to convert the pain into pleasure. Because when he rubs between my legs, I feel my pussy thumping.

He settles between my legs and lifts my body up to meet his, the tip of his cock at my entrance. Then he slowly burrows himself deep inside me, making me gasp for air.

"Oh … so fucking good." He smacks my ass again as he thrusts in and out, and my body tenses from the truckload of sensations hitting me.

In and out, so far, so deep. It feels so full … so good.

As he hits the spot, my eyes roll into the back of my head, and I almost come.

Right then, he takes a fistful of my hair and pulls my head back, making me hiss.

"Did I say you could come?"

"No."

"Bad girl." He spanks me again, and it makes me bite my pillow. "You come when I say. You understand?"

"Yes."

Another slap follows. "Louder!"

"Yes!"

He grunts, and the sound is so sexy I struggle to compose myself. As he keeps thrusting, I feel myself getting wetter and wetter, feeling the need to let go. Maybe this is what I needed. Finally, I can give myself to someone without feeling bad. Without feeling guilt. Without ... anything. My mind is blank.

He pulls his dick out and spanks my ass two times before rubbing my pussy fast. "Come. Now."

I don't know why, but his slick, dark voice and touch make me explode. And as I drown in my own orgasm, he taps my pussy, intensifying it even more.

Panting, I struggle to breathe, but he flips me over anyway.

"My turn."

Before I know it, he's shoved his cock into my mouth with no warning. He goes deep. Far. Thick. I can taste myself as well as him on my tongue, and I cough from his length.

"Take it deep," he growls, pushing even farther.

Only when I'm almost out of breath does he pull out to allow me some air.

And back in again he goes, fucking me right in my face.

I can feel his balls slapping against my chin as he grasps my head and forces me to take him all the way. Exactly as I remember. Just as powerless as I felt back then. But this time, it's different. This time, it's a controlled situation I can get out of any time I want. Something I chose. And slowly but surely, the memory starts to fade and all that's left is Drake fucking me like I asked him to.

As he pulls out, I gasp and say, "More."

"More?" He laughs.

I nod, as he pumps into my mouth again.

"I'll give you more," he growls, pinching my nose. "Can you feel it?" His cock pulses in my throat, and I gurgle as I try to nod again. "Fuck."

With one hand, he holds my head and shoves it over his cock, while the other hand is rubbing my clit again. I'm being overloaded with sexual need, and I feel like I could come, cry, and laugh at the same time.

Tears roll down my cheeks from his rough face fucking, but I don't regret it for even one second as he fiercely rubs my pussy. All I feel is the need to do whatever he wants and succumb to ecstasy.

"Yes. Come, Hyun," he growls.

And as he pleasures me, I fall apart with him inside me.

Right as he jets his seed into the back of my throat.

He holds my face as my eyes dart around in a frenzy. "Swallow."

Thick juices lie on my tongue, and I swallow it all back. More spurts down as he thrusts in again, his cock hard and pulsing, his eyes greedily looking down upon me, the look on his face one of raw need.

I watch him release all his pent-up energy inside

me, coming to a panting stop. When he's sated, he pulls himself out of my mouth and releases my pussy from his grip. We're both out of air but not out of stares ... and ours are saying words we cannot say out loud.

With his thumb, he swipes along my lips and gently sticks it into my mouth. I suck, and he murmurs, "Now, your memories are mine."

Goose bumps scatter on my skin as I mumble, "Thank you."

He knows why I say it.

Nothing else needs to be said.

He unties my wrists and lies down in bed beside me, wrapping his arm around my waist and pulling me close to his side.

It's silent for a few seconds, and I use the opportunity to ask him something that's been on my mind for quite some time now. "Why did you ... write that you wanted to wrap your fingers around my neck?"

It takes him a while to answer. His voice is thick and low ... making me shiver. "You know why."

I know why ... because I am his.

He had known it before I did.

Together until death. That's what he wants. What I need.

Someone who will take me away from Greg forever, in whatever way necessary.

He buries his face in my neck and presses a soft

kiss to my skin.

"There's only one thing we can do to stop Greg forever ..." he whispers into my ears.

I nod, a tear falling down my cheeks. I'm not sad. I'm relieved.

"Yes," I answer, knowing full well he's right.

It's time to end this all.

21

Hyun

A few days later

I take a deep breath before I knock on my parents' door. I haven't seen them in ages. In fact, the last time was on my wedding day. I always wondered why they never came to visit me when I lived with Greg. Then again, I already knew the answer. They didn't care. They had their money, and I had a good home ... or so they thought. It didn't matter to them what I felt.

And as my mom opens the door and I see the surprised look on her face, I know for a fact she still doesn't want to care.

"Hyun?" Her face turns into a complete sour mess.

"What are you doing here? We've tried to reach you for ages. Where's Greg?"

I purse my lips and straighten my body. "I left him."

Her eyes widen. "What?" she scoffs.

"Who is that, honey?" my dad asks in Korean, but as he comes to the door, his jaw drops too. "Hyun. Why are you here?"

"I'm great, Dad, thanks for asking." I give them a fake smile. "I just wanted to visit you. You know ... because we haven't seen each other in such a long time."

"Well, aren't you with Greg now?" Dad asks.

"No, they split," Mom interjects. Dad frowns, looking upset.

Mom grabs my arm and holds on tight. "Why?"

"You know *exactly* why." I jerk my arm free. "I never liked him. He used me. Hit me. He's an awful person, and you knew it."

"Nonsense." My mom makes a face. "He was always a gentleman around us. I don't get where this is coming from. And why couldn't you come visit sooner? Maybe bring him along too. It would've been so nice."

"Because you never cared enough to visit me either, even though you knew what you'd done to me," I hiss.

She swallows; visibly shaken from the realization that not everything is as great as the pretty picture she painted in her head.

"Why don't you come inside so we can talk?" Dad asks.

"No, thanks," I say. "I just wanted to know ... Did you ever really love me?"

"What kind of question is that? Of course, honey!" Mom replies.

I hold up my hand. "No, Mom. I mean for real. You sold me to a man like I was something to own. How could you?" Tears well up in my eyes, but she doesn't reply. All I'm faced with are silent stares, and it says enough. "Don't you have anything to say?" With my voice faltering, I beg for a response ... anything ... to make what I've been through less of a persecution. But they give me nothing. Just as they have all those years.

"Right ..." I cringe. "Why would I ever expect anything from you?"

As I turn around, Mom grabs my hand. "Wait. Please stay. We only wanted you to have a good life."

"A good life?" The words sound hollow ... and filthy.

"We thought he'd be good for you," Dad says.

"Because he gave you money. That made him trustworthy?" I snap.

"Because he told us so," Dad says.

"I still believe he could be the right man for you. Maybe you two just need some help."

"What?" My jaw drops. "Mom. He *physically* hurt me. Degraded me. Yelled at me."

The look in her eyes still tells me she doesn't believe what I say.

"I had to run for my life to get away from him," I say. "Why don't you believe me instead of him?"

"I don't know ..." She shakes her head. "I can't ..."

A tear rolls down my cheeks. "And still you want me to return to him."

"If only you understood him, maybe then he would be nice," she says. "He could give you so much. Why would you leave him? Maybe if you went back, everything would be okay."

"No, Mom, nothing would be okay. I would *not* be okay." I'm holding the doorframe for support, anything to ground me because right now it feels like I'm sinking into a black, bottomless pit.

"I *hate* him," I hiss.

"I don't believe that," Dad says. "There must be *something* good about him."

"Stop," I say, my voice getting louder. "Just stop. I came here to see if you'd finally regretted your decision, but I was wrong to believe you'd ever change." My fingernails dig into the wood.

"You needed money, so you sold me. Tell me. Say it to my face that you did that."

"Yes, we sold you to Greg."

I swallow when I finally hear her admission. "Was I ever more than just a money tree to you?"

"If you'd gone to a university and become a lawyer,

we wouldn't have had to," Mom says.

"Or a doctor," Dad adds as if it makes it any better that he offers me options.

"You wouldn't want a daughter who worked at a coffee shop. Of course," I say, blinking away the remaining tears.

"We sold you to him because the marriage would make you a better person," Mom says.

"You think so too?" I ask Dad, looking him directly in the eyes.

Neither of them shows any remorse. "Yes."

That's it.

The final bullet tore through my heart.

I nod slowly with a scowl on my face, releasing the doorframe from my grip. "Fine. This is the last time you'll ever see me again."

As I turn around and start to walk, Mom yells at me. "What about Greg?"

"You won't see him either."

"But … Hyun!" Dad tries to call me back, but I keep on walking.

"No," I yell back, finally feeling like I've done something good. Something solely for me. "I gave you your final chance. It's over."

***

DRAKE

I pick up my ringing phone and answer it when I'm sure no one's listening in to the conversation.

"It's done." Hyun's voice makes my head fill with worries.

"I talked to them," she continues. "They finally said exactly what I wanted to hear. So now I'm done with them forever."

"But they're your parents ..."

"No," she says. "It's over. I don't need them anymore."

The phone call ends in beeps, and I look down at my cell phone and realize she's finally come to her senses. A proud smile spreads on my lips.

A half an hour later, I'm at her home, and when I knock on the door and she opens it, I'm met with open arms and a hug. "Are you okay?" I ask.

"No." She sniffs and sucks in a few breaths. "But I will be."

"If you want me to—"

"Tomorrow. We'll deal with it tomorrow. Stay the night, please." Her pleading voice is like music to my ears. "I need you close."

"Of course," I answer. "What about ...?" I don't dare finish my sentence. I don't want to upset her. However, I get the feeling she knows exactly what I mean.

She tilts her head back to look at me, swiping away a tear that rolled down her cheek. "I'm ready."

"Are you sure?" I ask, looking at her with half-mast eyes. "There's no taking it back. Once they're out of your life, they're out."

She nods, her face turning resolute ... bold ... different from what I've seen before. She's changed since I've been here. Whether it's for the better, we'll have to find out.

"All right," I say. "But first, let's eat."

She licks her lips and walks back into the kitchen, taking a soufflé out of the oven. "Made it just for this special occasion." She puts it on the table and points at a chair. "Sit."

It's been a long time since someone invited me to dinner ... and a long time since I actually listened to someone when they gave me a command. But for her, I'd gladly do anything. And when it comes to her food, nothing can beat the taste.

I take in the scent of delicious cheese. "Yum."

She grabs our plates and scoops it up for us, after which she pours wine into our glasses and holds up her glass. We toast. "To a better future," she says with a smile.

"May they all rot in hell," I add, and she returns my

grin.

Right as she puts down her glass and I pick up my fork, she pulls something from her pocket and places it on the table. The audio recorder I gave her.

"Listen," she says, as she plays the recording of her conversation with her parents. "Do you hear it?"

I bite my lip, and a lopsided smile forms on my lips. "The sound of humiliation and defeat."

She cocks her head, the vengeful look in her eyes finally culminating to what it should have been all this time. "Exactly."

***

Accompanying Song: "I Started A Joke" by ConfidentialMX ft. Becky Hanson

A few days ago

As she lies in my arms, dozing off into a soundless sleep, my eyes remain open. I think about my past and the one thing I haven't told her yet, wondering if I should. It's something important, something that made me who I am. But it was wrong. So wrong. And I regret it to this very day.

I've never told a single soul.

But she ... she's worth it.

And I wanna find out if she can carry the burden of

knowing the truth.

So I clutch her shoulder and whisper in her ear, "Can I tell you a secret?"

"Mmmhmm," she mumbles, half-asleep.

I smile against her skin and press a kiss to her neck. "It's about the girl from my class ... when I was still a teacher."

"What about her?" Her eyes flicker open.

"I didn't take it so well that she betrayed me," I say, caressing her neck and shoulder. "So I went to her house ... and strangled her with her own scarf."

Her eyes burst open, and she stares ahead at the wall, not moving an inch.

I wait, but there's no response, so I softly ask, "Are you afraid of me?"

She shakes her head. "No."

I lick my lips and place another kiss on her shoulder. "Even when you know I'm a killer?"

"I would've done the same thing," she replies.

In disbelief, I stare at her for a few seconds then shake my head and swallow a laugh.

I give her a final kiss on the cheek and lie down, closing my eyes. "Good night."

***

Hyun

Now

I dream of the city and blood raining from the sky. It's a dream within a dream, but I can't wake up, no matter how hard I try. And through it all ... I carry a witch-like smile.

When I finally wake up, Drake is gone. I'm not surprised.

I rise and put on some clothes, rinsing my face before going into the kitchen to make some coffee. But on the counter, I find something that stops me in my tracks. A camera.

I don't own a camera like this.

Frowning, I pick it up and check the images on the SD card, wondering if Drake left it here. But then I notice the pictures he shot are of me. All of them. Including ones where I'm in my bed ... under the shower ... naked.

All of them.

Explicit as can be.

22

Accompanying Song: "Technically, Missing" by Trent Reznor & Atticus Ross

Hyun

My hands shake, and I clutch the counter to remain standing as I come face to face with my own image. I know Drake always had a thing for me. I know he was watching me every single minute of the day. But I never knew it went this far. This deep.

And now, I wonder why he left it here for me to find.

Does he want me to keep them or destroy them?

Only one choice fits this narrative.

With trembling fingers, I peel open the back of the camera and take out the SD card. I go to my bedroom and fish the folder from underneath my bed, stuffing the SD card in with all the other notes Drake has sent me. It's safe here. No one knows where I keep these except me.

Like a little secret we share that no one can find out about.

Just him and me.

For better ... or for worse.

Only when I go back into the kitchen do I notice the small piece of paper lying on the counter. On it are a few typed out words that create knots in my stomach. But still, as I read through it over and over again, I bring it to my folder and stuff it inside, knowing full well what the message entails ... and that I'm about to keep it.

There was once a man who loved a woman so deeply he would die for her.

But no matter what he did, he couldn't make her happy. Not as long as other people kept her from him. People who didn't understand their type of love.

So in order to be together forever ... the man concocted a plan.

And decided to end it ... once and for all.

***

DRAKE

I put on the suit I've kept in my closet for weeks and look at myself in the mirror to make sure everything looks exactly the way it's supposed to. Then I put on a hat, grab the rope on the counter, and leave my home. Jogging through the woods, I make sure no one sees me as I put on my gloves and make my way to the city.

Being as inconspicuous as possible is my forte, and even if people see me, I know they won't recognize me. I'm wearing a fake mustache, and combined with the hat and the clothes, I look like a whole different person.

Exactly what I need to get the job done.

I trek the way to my destination on foot. To make sure I can't be tracked here, I'm not using my car or any other vehicle. When I finally arrive at the house, my heart begins to race, and a wicked smile forms on my lips. I've waited so long to be able to do this, and now that the moment has finally arrived ... I feel like a kid trick-or-treating on Halloween night.

With big steps, I walk up to the porch and make sure no one's around before knocking on the door and swiftly hiding behind one of the bushes. The door creaks open, and I hear footsteps.

"Hello?" a sweet voice utters, but I know she's a devil in sheep's clothing.

I don't respond. I wait. And when she turns around to close the door, I lunge inside.

Within a second, I have the rope wrapped around her neck.

Twisting.

Turning.

Her hands grasp at the fiber. Nails desperately trying to claw their way out.

I hiss, "This is it ... This is the end."

"Help ..." Her voice is scratchy. The harder I pull, the better it sounds.

"No one's coming to help you now. You never helped *her* either."

"Hyun ...?" She gasps, and I know she realizes exactly why I'm here.

"You brought this upon yourself," I growl into her ear, pulling the rope even tighter.

Her skin breaks underneath the fibers. She struggles so much that it feels empowering. Invigorating.

Exquisite.

Like tasting a fine wine from an age-old bottle.

Or the first rain after a drought.

Or like the smile on your lover's face after seeing her languish in lasting misery.

My blood rushes with fury and contempt as I pull the string tighter and tighter until there's no more room for breath. Until her lips stop producing sound. Until her arms grow limp and her body collapses in my arms.

Death.

A bittersweet revenge.

A voice calls from upstairs in a language unfamiliar to me.

I drop her body, the sound of it flopping onto the floor not even fazing me as I walk into the kitchen and grab the biggest butcher's knife I can find. Then I wait behind the door as the man saunters down the stairs. I hear his footsteps as they barge into the hallway and come to a soundless halt.

I know why he stopped.

He's witnessing the unraveling of his whole life.

And nothing about it matters because I approach him from behind, reach around, and shove the knife deep into his throat.

He gurgles out loud as he sees the dead body of his wife and knows his own demise is near.

Blood spouts out like a broken faucet, and the man immediately grabs his neck in an attempt to stop the bleeding. He realizes too late that the blade is still stuck in his flesh ... and that my hand is holding it in place.

As he stumbles in place, I pull it out and ram it back in below his ribs. Again. And again. Until his body slumps to the floor, convulsing, blood pouring everywhere.

I look down upon my victim and cock my head, wondering what he's trying to say, but nothing manages to come out from between his lips … except for blood.

I go to my knees beside him, gazing into his soulless eyes, which beg me to relieve him of his pain. But I will do no such thing. Instead, I take my time to wipe the blood off the knife on his shirt, his body jolting up and down from each stroke. I clean the knife thoroughly and tuck it into my pocket.

With grinding teeth, I growl, "This … this is all on you. If only you had loved your daughter more than you did."

And then I get up and walk out the door, tipping my hat to make sure it covers my face as I get out of there.

***

I take out my prepaid cell phone and dial Greg's fucking number. When he finally picks up, the first and only thing I say is, "I just fucked her real good. You jealous?"

Then I hang up the phone, take out the chip, crush it, and chuck everything in a bin beside the road.

A smug smile spreads across my lips as I imagine the asshole exploding in rage. Magnificent.

Fifteen minutes later and I'm at *his* home.

I've waited for so long to finally see him burn.

First, I put my gloves back. Then, after I've made sure no one's around, I sneak up under his window and peer inside. I don't see anyone there, so I jerk the window to see if it's unlocked. Luckily, it is, and I scoot it open enough to be able to slip through.

With mouse steps, I glide through the house, looking around every corner before I go to the next room. I don't want to get caught, but it doesn't look like anyone's home.

It doesn't faze me at all.

I go into his kitchen and open the drawers until I find one filled with cutlery and place the knife inside. I rummage in my other pocket and take out the two pictures I made of Hyun, placing them on the counter. One of the notes I typed out is carefully placed beside his laptop sitting on the counter. I open his laptop and open a word file, typing out a few more words that look exactly like the messages I've sent to Hyun so far, and save it to his files. Then I take out the audio recorder Hyun used and place it in the drawer beside the knife.

Before I leave, I grab his packet of cigarettes lying on the cabinet in the hallway and light one up. Nothing beats smoking a good cigarette while escaping a motherfucker's house. Except for a neatly fitting crime scene that's perfectly shaped for destruction.

***

Hyun

Accompanying Song "My Body" by Perfume Genius

When the doorbell rings and someone slams the door obsessively, I know it's about to go down.

"Hyun? Open the goddamn door!" It's him. I knew it. Greg.

With a knot in my stomach, I grab the gun hidden behind the vase, determined not to let him corner me again. It's time I ended this game of cat and mouse once and for all.

When I was still with him, I always loathed myself for not sticking up for myself. For not fighting him more. For not doing everything I should have, sooner . . .

But now, finally, I'm coming into my true self. The person I want to be.

And I won't rely on anyone to save me.

With the gun in my hand, I stalk toward the door and listen.

"YOU FUCKING BITCH, OPEN THE FUCKING DOOR!"

I don't think I've ever heard him yell this loud.

He rams the door so hard I can see the wood crack.

"You lying whore, fucking another man. I knew it!"

217

Right as he's ranting, I pull open the door and hold up the gun, hoping to shoot him down. However, as I'm aiming and trying to pull the trigger, he manages to ram me like a bull, bulldozing me back inside my own house. He pushes me against the wall, pinning my wrist in a place that makes me drop the gun to the floor.

"Let go!" I scream.

"You fucking bitch, how dare you?!" He's screaming so loud it's like my ears pop.

Instinct drives me to protect myself, and as he puts his hand on my throat, I kick him straight in the nuts. I run into my bathroom but not in time to slam the door shut. He chases me, jerking the door from my grip and shoving me against the tiled wall.

I claw at his face, but it's no use; he won't stop. With a hand on my wrist and a hand on my mouth, he hisses, "You're not getting away this time."

I do the only thing I can at this point and bite him as hard as I can. Through his flesh … I can taste his blood in my mouth.

He howls at the top of his lungs, pulling away immediately, after which he smacks me so hard I land face-first against the shower wall. However, I use the opportunity to my advantage and grab the showerhead, swiftly pulling the hose over his neck. I pull, hard, tightening the metal wire around his neck until I hear him choke.

"You motherfucker … you've hurt me for the last goddamn time," I growl, putting all my strength into wrapping the hose around his neck.

"Stop ..." He gurgles, reaching for the hose.

I twist the knot tighter in response. "No."

I don't stop.

Not as he begs me to.

Not as he tries to claw his way back into life.

Not as he breathes his final breath.

His body sinks to the ground and takes me with it. Still clutching the shower hose, I breathe in and out steadily, sweat drops rolling down the back of my neck from my ordeal.

I push his filthy body off me and crawl up from the floor. I don't look back, not even once before I make my way to the telephone and dial 911.

"This is 911, what's your emergency?"

I clutch the phone with both hands, my brain going on autopilot. "I killed my husband."

23

Accompanying Song: "What Have We Done To Each Other" by Trent Reznor & Atticus Ross

DRAKE

Two hours after Greg's murder

From behind a tree, I look at the house through my binoculars. I'm far enough not to draw any attention to myself but close enough to watch the scene unfold. Two ambulances and three police cars arrive one at a time. The first two medics went inside and never came out. Not until five others, including three policemen, join the group.

A medic escorts Hyun out of her house to be checked out in one of the ambulances. They help her clean off the blood and tend to her wounds, placing a soft blanket over her shoulders. She weeps, consoling herself by hugging the blanket close, and it's at that moment that I feel most ashamed. I should've been there. I should be the one to hug her and tell her it's going to be okay. But I know I can't. It would ruin everything we fought so hard to achieve.

So I stay and watch as the coroner arrives and goes inside. Minutes later, a body is hauled outside on a stretcher, tucked away into a body bag to mask the damage done by the scorned wife.

I knew she had it in her.

She went through so much suffering, so much pain at his hand. Even after escaping his house, she could not escape his terror. And I knew when I saw her ... one day ... she would break. And that day was now.

***

A few days later

With a cup of coffee, I sit down on the couch in my cabin and turn on the television. A news report catches my attention, and I stop drinking my coffee to listen to what the reporter has to say.

"A woman murdered her husband after he came into her house and attacked her. Witnesses have stated her husband has been stalking her for the past few weeks after she'd left him in a desperate attempt to save herself. Insiders report the husband having scratch marks all over his face, saying he was suffocated by a shower hose after what appeared to be a struggle. The woman has bruises all over her body and is now at the hospital."

I take a quick sip from my coffee and put it down on the table, listening carefully.

"Police have found several pieces of evidence suggesting the man was sending her illicit notes, including threats. There's currently an ongoing investigation at the man's house as well as the woman's house. Sources claim several pictures of her taken without her knowledge were found in his home, along with an audio tape of her parents saying they forced her to marry the man. The outrageous story continues as, only minutes ago, the police found two dead bodies in her parents' home. Whether these are her parents have yet to be confirmed. However, in a statement made to the media, the woman herself claims not to have killed them."

I pick up my lighter and grab a cigarette, lighting one up as I watch the story unfold.

"This just came in. Police reports show a bloody knife was found at the husband's house. Whether the blood belongs to the victim's parents has yet to be verified."

As I take a drag of my cig and blow out the smoke, I can't help but smile.

***

Hyun

Social workers.

Police.

Reporters.

Medical people.

They all come and go, asking for the same information over and over again. I repeat my story to all, remembering as much as I can while leaving out as little as possible. It never changes. Not a tiny fleck in my convincing tale.

Every time they talk to me, I swipe away a few tears, sniffling into a handkerchief I'm given before the conversation, like they know I will cry. As any person in my situation, one is expected to be a victim. To act like a victim. To become the victim.

In order to win.

I play my part and smile when they are kind, and suck my lip and form tears in my eyes when they mention the pain I've endured. A few nods and distant stares are all that's needed to make them believe.

The whole world knows my story by now.

I even talked to the press myself, though briefly. I masqueraded as being too weak to feel up to the task of answering all their questions, and it worked in my favor.

After all the questions and the fiddling with my body, I finally learn the outcome of my ordeal from my lawyer. I only listen with half my brain as I stare off into the distance, wondering if the world even realizes what's unfolding here.

I've been declared a victim and will not be facing any charges.

What I did has been labeled an act of self-defense.

I am a woman getting off scot-free with the criminal act of murdering her husband.

I cry tears of joy. They spring into my eyes as if they come naturally. As if I'm not at all miserable inside after what this man has done to me. But I returned the viciousness a thousandfold.

And as the people kiss me on the cheek and congratulate me on my freedom, I feel melancholic. Not in the present.

All I can think about is what the future will hold.

With the press following my every footstep, I go outside. Hidden underneath a dark blanket, I'm trying to hide from the world. But everyone already knows my story. They know it better than I do.

I get into the car and quickly take off the blanket, feeling suffocated by it. Luckily, the tinted windows make it impossible for others to see the true me. Until my lawyer, Lauren Banning, gets into the car with me and asks, "Are you okay?"

"Mmmhmm." I nod, licking my lips as I stare at the

photographers.

"They can't see you through the glass."

"I know."

"Do you want to go home?" she asks.

I nod. "But I'm not staying there."

"I know," Lauren says. "You already told me."

"Right." I smile at her.

"Where will you be going?"

"I don't know," I say, shrugging. "Anywhere but here."

"I hope it's some place safe," she says.

"It is," I muse, trying not to give her too much info, even though she's fishing.

"And with someone who's safe," she adds.

I ignore that last statement as if I don't know what she's talking about.

Of course, rumors floated around that I was having an affair. That I had not one but three boyfriends. That I was a hooker and my husband traded me. All kinds of stories follow a woman who has murdered her husband … because no husband deserves such a cruel death, right? That's what they want to believe, anyway, but I know the truth.

And I've been set free.

They don't know anything.

They only know what I want them to know.

When the car arrives at my house, my lawyer steps out first while I cover my face with a blanket. So many reporters are outside that the moment I open my door it feels like a tide rolling in from the high seas pushes me back in. But I persist and wade through the crowd with her help until we finally get to my door and go inside.

The clicking sounds of cameras and the yelling reporters cut off like a sudden vacuum in space as she shuts the door and closes all the curtains. My whole body feels numb as I walk through this house again … for the first time since I killed *him*.

Instinctively, I walk into the bathroom, as if I'm expecting to find his body still lying there on the cold, hard floor, white eyes staring back at me. Of course, it's a fantasy. There's nothing here. Absolutely nothing. Not even a tiny hair or a speck of blood.

"Are you sure you're all right?"

Lauren's sudden voice makes me jolt, and I clear my throat and turn around. "Yeah. I'm fine." I give her a fake smile. I want nothing more than to get out of here, but I know those reporters would follow me wherever I go, so I have to lay low for now.

"It's so noisy outside," I say, trying to change the topic.

"Give it a few days. Once they realize you're not going to give them any more juicy details, they'll leave."

"Right," I say. "Thanks. For everything." We shake hands.

"Don't mention it," she says. "Well, if you need anything, you know where to find me. Or call." She chuckles awkwardly.

"Of course."

She picks up her briefcase and walks toward the door, but before she goes outside, she says, "Be careful, okay?"

I nod, not knowing what to say to such a thing.

I know she worries about me, and it comes from a good place. She's a good woman. I've not met many like her before. I smile as she says goodbye and leaves me. All alone. In the house that held a corpse.

In the house where I'll bury all my secrets and turn them to dust.

Part IV
The Scheme

24

Accompanying Song: "What Have We Done To Each Other" by Trent Reznor & Atticus Ross

Hyun

One week later

"Well, Miss Warr—I mean Song," the notary says, almost choking on his words. "I'm glad to tell you that at least one positive thing came out of everything you've been through." He grabs a few pieces of paper lying on the stack on his desk and holds them out to me. "It's all yours."

"What …?" I mutter, leaning over the papers, pretending I can't believe my eyes.

"I'm happy to report that it is. Since Mr. Warren never signed the divorce papers, you were never actually divorced. Thus, you are now the rightful owner of his estate as well as his bank accounts."

I lick my lips as I go over the words on the paper, again and again, my eyes lingering on my name written in bold under the official notification from the bank that says I am now the owner.

"Like I said ... it's all yours."

"Mine. No one will take it away from me?" I ask him, looking him straight in the eyes.

"Well, a few expenses still need to be deducted, namely the costs of his funeral and—"

"Funeral?" I cringe.

"Yes."

"I don't want to ..."

"I understand if you would not wish to attend, but we still need to bury him," he explains. "As well as your parents, of course."

"Oh ... I see."

He clears his throat. "I apologize, that was a little insensitive of me."

I shake my head. "No, it's okay."

He gently smiles. "I will make arrangements to let the funeral commence without your presence."

"Thank you," I say. "I want nothing to do with it."

He nods. "About the expenses ... legal fees will also be deducted."

"I understand," I interrupt. "But after that ...?"

He nods with a smile on his face. "All yours."

I try not to laugh.

I honestly do.

But I still can't stop the wicked grin from spreading on my lips.

***

Accompanying Song: "What Have We Done To Each Other" by Trent Reznor & Atticus Ross

A few days later

It's raining cats and dogs as I stand above my parents' grave, watching their caskets get covered with dirt. I don't know what to feel. I just stand there, empty, staring at the soil.

When all is said and done, I place a final flower on top of the mound and nod as people ask me if I'm okay. We go into the building to drink coffee and eat cookies, which is, of course, the normal thing to do after you saw two dead bodies being lowered into the ground.

You eat cookies.

Even if you're sick to your stomach, you must eat the damn cookies.

And it gives others the time to tell you how sorry they are for you like that's useful in any way.

As I sit on a not-so-relaxing chair, eating that damn cookie, Annushka approaches me. I knew she was here,

I saw her from the corner of my eye as my parents were buried, but I didn't give it much thought as to *why* she was here.

"Hey," she says, licking her lips like she doesn't know what to say. "I'm ... sorry for your loss."

"Thank you," I say, taking a deep breath.

She places a hand on my shoulder but quickly pulls it away again after she probably realizes it's really weird. "I just wanted to say I'm sorry for what Greg did to you."

I frown as it feels like knots form in my stomach. "You talked about me to your husband. He knew everything about me because of you. Where I lived. Who I was seeing."

"I know, and I'm sorry." She makes a face and bites her lip. "I don't know what to do to make it up to you."

I look down at the table and sigh. "You don't have to do anything," I say.

She sighs out loud. "I feel so bad. He just ..."

I look up at her. "Forced you to do it?"

She nods slowly. "After he found out I helped you escape Greg's home, he forced me to give him all the details of our conversations, or else he'd make my life more miserable. I didn't want to but ..."

I grab her hand and squeeze. "I know how it feels." She doesn't have to say it out loud. I know what being threatened feels like, and it makes you do things you don't want to, just to protect yourself.

I smile gently, and her mood seems to improve.

Funny. We're at my parents' funeral, and I'm the one comforting others. It's a little ironic.

"Thank you," she says as she pulls her hand back. She turns her head and looks at her husband, who taps his feet and seems pissed that he even has to wait for her. "Well, I'm gonna go now."

"Thanks for coming," I say.

"Don't mention it. If you ever need someone to talk to ... now that Greg is gone," she says, chuckling. "I'm here."

I nod and smile as she turns around and leaves. "Good luck, Annushka."

She only briefly glances over her shoulder after my comment.

Nothing else needs to be said. She knows exactly why I told her good luck. It's not easy living with a man like that. I know.

I grab my coffee and chug it down in one go then get up to leave.

"Leaving already?" my aunt asks.

"No, I'm just going to take a breather outside," I reply.

"Oh. Of course," she says, smiling as I walk past her and go outside.

The pouring rain hits my skin hard, but I welcome the cold. It's refreshing. After a day like this, it feels cleansing.

I step farther out and walk through the cemetery,

admiring the melancholic beauty of the stones surrounding me. My hair turns to sticky webs against my skin, but the cold touch is exactly what I need to cool down.

However, when I see a dark figure disappear behind a tree after looking my way, I know my cool down is about to come to an abrupt stop.

***

Accompanying Song: "Burning Desire" by Lana Del Rey

DRAKE

The moment I see her, I know I've been caught.

Our eyes connect, and I immediately turn around and hide behind the tree.

My heart is pounding, and I lick my lips from just the anticipation that I'll finally see her again.

I know curiosity prevents her from walking away.

She always has to know why I'm here.

Always needs to be just that little step closer.

I swiftly walk behind a different tree and watch her approach the one I was behind. Her clothes are soaked from the rain, making her look even more appetizing than normal. I'm unable to stop myself from pouncing on her.

Exactly when she doesn't see me coming.

From behind, I stalk up to her and push her against the tree. With my hand, I block her mouth, while my other holds her down.

"Don't scream," I whisper in her ear, my tongue darting out to have a quick taste.

She softly shakes her head, but her eyes are wild.

"What are you doing here?" she murmurs through my hand.

"Watching you …" I say, looking into her eyes to see her reaction.

My lips can't stop themselves from pressing a kiss onto her skin, though. Her head leans back onto my shoulder, almost as if she wants me to kiss her.

My hand grips her waist and snakes its way up her wet shirt, curling it up so I can grasp her tit and squeeze. She moans when I twist her nipple.

"You knew I was here …" I whisper. "Say it."

"I knew it," she says with a hampered breath through my hand.

"And still, you came closer," I murmur, planting another kiss below her ear.

"I needed to know …"

My hand now dives downward, pushing its way through the fabric of her pants to reach into her panties. Everything is soaked—even her pussy—and I grunt with excitement.

"You needed to know if I was really here?" I toy with her clit, twirling my finger around it, playing with her emotions and her arousal. I love the sight of her face as she loses control in my arms, unable to stop it.

Trapped between my arms against a tree in the soaking rain, she has nowhere to go, and I have dirty plans involving her. But does she still want me after everything that happened?

I remove my hand from her mouth, hoping she won't make a sound.

"I killed your parents," I murmur into her ear, ripping away the button of her jeans and unzipping her.

"I know," she replies, still moaning as I rip down her panties.

"Are you scared of me?" I growl, thrusting my fingers up her pussy.

No words. Nothing except soft moans and eyes that roll into the back of her head.

I know exactly how to play her.

How to make her do exactly what I want her to do.

"I'm a killer, Hyun," I growl into her ear, pinning her harder against the tree. "And I want to fuck your brains out."

I rip down my zipper and pull my dick out without even taking the trouble of pulling down my jeans. I'm so damn hard right now, and I need to be inside her.

So I grab her wrists, pin them together, and push my cock against her entrance.

"We're in a cemetery," she mutters.

"I don't fucking care. My cock fucking wants you, and it's going to claim you *now*."

I push deep, burying myself in her wet pussy. And god, does it feel good.

Like an animal, I fuck her from behind. Hard. Fast. Beastly. With no remorse or regret.

And I fucking love how wet she is for me. How, after all this, I can still fuck her because she's mine and mine alone.

Her skin is so damn wet from the rain; my tongue dips out to lick the drops off her skin. She moans softly, and I take it as a sign to start rubbing her again.

It feels so wrong, fucking in a cemetery, but it's hot too, in a kinky way. I pound into her, pumping all my pent-up rage into her. I can't control myself anymore, and I wouldn't even want to at this point. All I want is to watch her come. And when she does … it's magnificent. So beautiful is that look of pure desperation washing over her, rain still splattering onto her skin.

I feel her muscles around my dick, squeezing, making me wanna come.

So I pull out and push her back down, forcing her to bend over. That's when I blow my load all over her naked pussy and ass. Groaning, I keep coming, all over her, squirting myself empty over her holes.

And it's the best fucking feeling in the world.

Panting, I push my dick back into my pants and pull up her panties. I press a kiss on her back, whispering, "Don't move."

She listens, staying put against the tree like a

beautiful flower leaning against it.

The water mixes with my juices in an ultimate mix of deliciousness. I swear that if I had my camera with me right now, I'd take a snapshot.

But for now, my memory will have to suffice.

I grab her hands and lift them, pulling them over her eyes. "Close your eyes and count to twenty."

"Why?"

"Just do it."

She starts counting, her voice soft but still audible. When I'm sure she can't see me, I smile and turn around, disappearing from the premises.

I know she'll probably hate me for leaving her there, but there's not much else I can do except leave. It's a cemetery, after all … not a place to be found alive. Or fucking.

All I can do is wait … wait until she makes the decision.

***

Hyun

Days later

I waited until the media and reporters in front of

my house were gone before I ever went out. It was too risky to try to leave, knowing they could follow me. So I staked out in that hellhole for a few more days, watching them from behind the curtains. Waiting until each and every one of them had left before I grabbed my things and stuffed it all into a big suitcase.

Now, it's finally time for my freedom. For the first time in my life, I can decide what I want to do without anyone telling me that it's wrong or that I should feel guilty.

But the first thing on my list isn't something I enjoy. Still, it must be done, for the sake of keeping up appearances.

With a fresh bouquet of flowers, I march along the pebble path, admiring the beautiful tombstones laid out on the terrain. I think about death and about how close I came. Too close.

In the distance stands a stone angel with a crown of flowers around her head, her fingertips touching each other as she rises up into the sky. I decide, there and then, that once it is my time … my grave will carry that tombstone.

I continue my stroll with my suitcase behind me, the small wheels making a lot of noise skidding on the path. Clutching the flowers close to my heart, I walk until I meet the name I was searching for.

Here lie Mr. and Mrs. Song. May they rest in peace.

I look down and take a deep breath, blowing out a sigh as I place the flowers on top of the mound. Mentally, I say my goodbyes and make a cross on my chest.

Then I spit on their graves.

Twice.

"I had sex at your funeral," I growl.

I turn and walk away, determined never to return.

When I get to the cemetery gate with my suitcase still in my hand, a car drives up the lane, and the window rolls down. A familiar face greets me.

"Get in."

I quickly run to the other side and jump in, shutting the door ... before grabbing Drake's face and kissing him harder than I ever have before.

"And here I thought you were mad at me," he says between my kisses, grinning stupidly.

"Are you crazy?" I muse. "I was the one who asked you to meet me here."

"No, but I was a little worried, seeing you walk up there with a bunch of flowers. I almost started wondering if you had regrets."

"Pfft ..." I raise a brow. "No way. I don't miss them. In fact, I'm glad they're gone. Along with that slimy asshole." A lopsided smile spreads on my lips as I throw my suitcase in the backseat and add, "Besides ... I was the one who asked you to kill them, remember?"

He nods, smiling back at me like he's impressed at my willpower. "And now …?"

I bite my lip and stare at him with half-mast eyes, teasing him with a kiss right under his lips. "Now, we go to the bank, skip town, and roll around in all the cash we could ever need."

25

Accompanying Song: "What Have We Done To Each Other" by Trent Reznor & Atticus Ross

Hyun

8 months before

In the corner of the coffee shop sits a man behind a laptop.

He isn't just a random, ordinary man with dark hair, wearing a thin, black coat and a red scarf.

This man comes here every day of the week.

More specifically, I've been told he's been coming here ever since I started working.

From the corner of my eye, I stare at him while making a chocolate latté, wondering why he's always so busy typing … It's like he never does anything else.

Type and drink coffee for hours on end. And then he disappears.

At times, I catch him staring at me, but I can never keep my eyes on him. I'm too embarrassed, too shy to even remotely acknowledge the fact that he may be here because of me.

It's never occurred to me that anyone would go to that length just to see me.

I'm an ordinary girl, doing an ordinary job.

And that man ... he is something else entirely.

On only two occasions did he come in with a book instead of a laptop. Both of them were about writing subjects and how to improve your plotting and writing style. I know because I squinted hard enough to see the title.

I'm that obsessed with finding out more about him.

I wonder what he writes. If it's something I could read one day. If it's something I've already read and never knew. If he's someone I should know.

"Why don't you go talk with him?" my coworker Jasmin asks.

"Shhh." I shove her with my elbow. "Not so loud."

"Afraid he'll hear you're just as interested in him?" She sticks out her tongue coyly when I give her a look.

"I'm working!" I hiss between my teeth, trying not to let anyone hear.

"With half a brain, yeah." Jasmin grins and chuckles a little when she sees the blush on my face. "Oh, c'mon. We all know you're swooning."

"What? He's just ... good looking. That's all."

"No, you like the silent types." She winks. "The emotional, gooey, shy types."

I roll my eyes. "He's not like that."

"Yes, he is. He never dares to talk to you even though you're both waiting for it. You don't want to admit it, but you two would be a perfect date."

"Fine." I squint at her to try to make her stay quiet, and she finally gets the message because she shrugs.

"Well, if you never take the leap, you'll never find out what he's all about."

She walks away and serves the other customers their coffee. Meanwhile, I'm stuck at the cappuccino device, thinking about what she said. She's right. Fantasizing never got me anywhere. It's time I took some action.

And as the time slowly crawls by, more and more customers start to leave. Except him. He always stays until closing time, and even though he's the one to see us close shop, we never get a chance to speak.

I'm always there ... and he is too ... We just never pushed past our boundaries to open our mouths and talk to each other.

And for some reason, somehow, after all the customers leave, I find the courage to go up to him. I sit down in front of him with my heart beating out of my chest, and a cup of steaming hot coffee scooted his way.

With a smile on my face, I look at him, waiting ...

until he raises his head and his intense blue eyes meet mine. For the very first time, we interact.

"Hi," I say, my cheeks glowing red.

"Um … hi," he mumbles.

His voice is perfect. Dark and delish and so soft.

I could listen to it all day, even if it was only these two words.

I push the coffee closer to him, and his hand reaches for it. Our fingers briefly touch, and a hot current flashes through me. I pull back instinctively, not knowing what to do.

"Thanks," he says, his smile genuine. Infectious.

He brings the cup to his mouth and takes a big gulp, and I watch him swallow it. I don't know why I'm gazing so obsessively at him. I feel like an idiot. Yet I can't shake this feeling he'd know exactly what I meant if I'd told him.

"It's on the house," I say.

He smiles again and says, "What's your name?"

"Hyun Song."

He cocks his head and gives me his hand. "Drake Bryant."

I grab his hand. His handshake is firm, powerful. His hand warm and one I don't want to release. When he does, my own hand feels empty. Void of something that should've been there from the start.

He clears his throat and closes his laptop.

"What were you writing?" I ask.

"Oh, nothing important."

"No, really, I wanna know," I say.

"Just articles for the newspaper I work for. It's a column."

"Really? You're a columnist?"

"Yes." He grins. "It's not great, but it pays the bills."

"No, I think it's fantastic. You can write about anything you like. And you must be really good at it. I mean you write so much when you're here." I clear my throat and try to pass off the awkwardness when I realize I've said something that outs him as an obsessive coffee shop visitor.

"It is great. That's true," he says.

He doesn't seem like a man of many words, but that's okay.

"So … your accent," he mumbles.

"Oh, I'm Korean," I say, blushing again.

"Your English is very good," he says.

"Thank you," I answer. "I do my best."

"Oh, I know."

He knows?

He knows.

Because he always watches me. Of course.

It's suddenly quiet again, and neither of us knows what to say.

I hide behind my hair and pretend not to be totally flustered.

"Hey ... um ... I've got to go." He grabs his laptop, stuffs it in his backpack, and gets up like he suddenly has somewhere he needs to be.

And as he gets up, I do too. I don't know why, but I feel like I ruined something, and if I let him go now … maybe it's ruined forever.

As he starts walking toward the door, a sudden urge to stop him takes over.

"Will you be back?" I call out.

He glances at me over his shoulder and gives me a lopsided smile that makes butterflies fly in my stomach.

"Always."

***

5.5 months before

Ever since I first had the guts to talk to him, things went uphill. He took me on numerous dates and kissed me after two weeks. I felt like I could float on air, and when he first took me back to his apartment not far from the city, we went all the way.

It wasn't the last time, of course.

We had sex many … many times.

Like now, when we're back from the restaurant, drunk on wine and love, and bumbling through the hallway because we both can't stay on our feet. We're wasted and laughing and having a good time, making out and fondling each other as we stumble our way to his door.

And as he turns on the lights and slams the door shut, I rip off his shirt and tear at his belt. He grins against my lips, fighting my shirt and panties equally hard to get them out of the way. His hands are all over me, and I love every inch of his skin against mine as we find our way to his bed, half-naked.

We have sex, and it is the best sex I've ever had.

Drake is perfect.

A man who understands me.

Who doesn't mind that my English isn't perfect.

Gives me what I need without asking for anything in return.

He listens to my stories about my work and my daily life without interrupting. It doesn't matter what I tell him, as long as I'm with him, he loves me.

There's only one thing he doesn't know.

One thing I couldn't bear to see him go through.

One simple thing … a meeting … between me, a wretched man, and my parents. A plan so devious it makes me cry, even after I just had sex with the man I love so much.

"What's wrong?" Drake asks, kissing my neck.

"Oh, it was just so intense," I lie.

I don't want him to worry.

At least, not for now.

I'm still safe, here in his arms. That's all that matters right now.

Drake leans away and opens his cabinet. I don't know what he does, but when he turns to me, he nudges me over to his side. And then he shows me the tiny box in his hand. "I wanted to do this for a while now, but I just didn't have the guts."

Tears roll down my cheeks as he opens the box and says, "Will you marry me?"

I can't believe this is happening right now.

Out of all the things that could happen … this is the cruelest of them all.

"Don't …" I shake my head.

The happy smile that was on his face disappears like a cloud hampering the sun's rays. It kills me to see it.

"Don't what?"

"I can't," I mumble, tears streaming down.

I can barely pronounce the words I want to say. It's too much.

"Why … you don't want to marry me?"

I grab his face and kiss him. "Yes, of course, I do." I kiss him again.

"Then take it," he says, pulling the ring out.

I push the ring back and close the box in his hands. "I can't."

"Why not?" He seems so upset, and it's entirely my fault.

I feel so bad. Now I have to break his heart.

I never wanted him to find out … Not this way.

"I … my parents, they …"

"What did they do?" He grabs my arms and forces me to look at him.

"They sold me to another man," I whisper, sniffing. "As a bride."

His eyes widen, and he sinks back into the bed; his body slumps like his spirit has left his body, and all that remains is meat and bones.

The box in his hands slowly slips from his fingers.

"You're getting married," he mumbles.

I nod. "I hate him. But they left me no choice in the matter. I had to flee their home to get out."

"Flee? I thought you had your own home. Where've you been all this time then?"

"I've been staying at the coffee shop. I couldn't go to my own home. They know exactly where I live. They'd be waiting for me there."

He frowns and makes a face. "You should've told me. You could've crashed here."

"Tell the man I love that I'm out of a house, and that a sick old man has paid money to make me his wife like a slave? I can't," I say in my best English. More tears well up in my eyes. "Don't you understand how humiliating this is? I didn't tell you because I couldn't face the thought ... and seeing you like this ..." I grab his arm, trying to reconcile, but he pulls it away. "It hurts."

"Don't," he says, sliding off the bed. "Who is it?"

"Gregory Warren," I reply.

He's quiet for a moment.

"I love you," I say. "I really do."

"Don't say that!" he yells. "If you do, run away with

me."

"I can't … He said he'd ruin the coffee shop if I did. I like my boss and my co-workers. There's no telling what he'd do to them. And my parents will kill me if they find out."

His face is that of pure misery, and it tears my heart into tiny, shriveled up pieces.

"Why didn't you tell me this sooner?"

"I just couldn't … break your heart," I mutter.

"It's only more broken. I thought I was the one to marry you."

"I'm sorry," I say. It's hopeless. I screwed up—big time.

He walks to the window and stares outside. It's quiet for some time before he speaks again. "You … care about them all more than you care about yourself," he mutters.

I look down at the sheets, numb from the realization that I can't escape the pain, no matter how much I try.

"You have to marry him," he repeats, still not looking at me.

I'm surprised he'd let me.

Surprised he realizes why I must.

"I have no choice," I say, getting out of the bed too. "And I know it's only a matter of time until he finds me and takes me."

I pick up my clothes and put them on, but he's not saying anything, so I grab the rest of my stuff and say,

"I'll leave."

"Promise me you'll do everything you can to fight him," he says. "And if you want me to, I'll help."

I nod when he finally looks my way.

"I will always love you," he adds. "Even if you don't want me to."

"I know." I lick my lips, trying to stop the tears from running again. "I love you too."

But before either of us can say another word, I run.

I run from the pain.

I run from the only man who ever loved me enough to let me go.

26

Accompanying Song: "Technically, Missing" by Trent Reznor & Atticus Ross

Hyun

4 months before

The first time I saw him again since we separated was at my wedding.

I never expected him to show up.

I didn't think he'd have the guts.

But there he is, right in front of me as I stare in disbelief.

"Nice dress," he says, smoking a cigarette.

"Thanks," I say, tears welling up in my eyes. "How've you been?"

He shrugs. "Great, considering the circumstances."

I nod a few times, not knowing how to react.

He sits down beside me on the bench and says, "Mind if I smoke?"

"Go ahead," I say, chuckling.

"What's so funny?"

"You're so different."

He frowns. "What does that mean?"

"I mean ... different ... from Greg." I look at him and see the change in his eyes. They're much more fiery than I remember. "He never asks me anything."

"Of course," Drake scoffs.

"You also never used to smoke," I add.

He squints. "Yeah? Bad habit." He takes another drag and blows out a big breath.

"Why did you come here?" I ask.

"To see you."

The blatant honesty in his words still has me breathless to this very day.

"Have *you* changed?" he suddenly asks.

"What do you mean?"

He cocks his head and puts his cigarette in his mouth as he speaks. "Are you still going through with it?"

I purse my lips and hold up my hand, showing him my ring finger.

"Right ..." He looks away.

"I still hate him with all my guts," I say.

"Yeah, well, if you ever get enough of him, you know where to find me." He gets up.

"Do I?" I ask before he starts walking.

He looks at me over his shoulder and says, "If you leave him, I will find you."

"And what then?" I raise a brow.

"Then … it's time we played a game with them."

I smirk. "What kind of game?"

He smirks right back. "If he hurts you, we'll hurt him twice as bad … and your parents too."

The smile on my face only widens. "I like the sound of that."

"Good. I'll know when you're ready to play." He turns and starts walking.

"How will I know?"

"Notes, Hyun. You know what my passion is," he answers with a grin. "Never forget… I'll always be watching you."

And that's the last I hear from the man in the hoodie.

My man.

My only man.

Drake Bryant.

***

Now

The stories we tell aren't always as clear-cut as they seem.

From the first time I saw him following me, I knew it was him.

As he sat on the bench across from my house.

As he appeared in front of me in the parking lot.

As he stalked me in my very own home.

I *always* knew it was him.

I just didn't know if, after all this time, he was still the same man.

If I could trust him. If he still loved me or if he hated me for what I'd done.

If he secretly worked with my husband to spite me.

Those were my fears ... the only ones ... and they were unfounded.

And as he began to send me notes, I was intrigued. I didn't know where it was going, but I knew it was something important. Something I had to keep close in case they became useful. And they did.

When my husband kept harassing me, all I could do was hope that Drake would protect me when the time came. Of course, I wanted Greg dead. However, I knew I would never be able to prove myself innocent if I killed him outright. So I didn't.

Instead, Drake's notes made it clear to me that we were on a different path.

One where we would forge our own story.

A story where a husband stalks his wife.

Repeatedly threatens her.

Leaves cigarettes in her bin.

Sends her indecent notes.

Wiretaps her to keep her in check.

Takes pictures of her and keeps them in his home.

Murders her parents when they tell her the truth about her marriage to him.

The neighbors went along so well, reporting they saw Greg banging my door and yelling at me repeatedly, even spotting him stalking me.

And every time I found a new piece of evidence placed by Drake so diligently, I went along with it. Even if I didn't know it ... like the cigarette. It was part of Drake's plan. Because who would believe a woman faking a surprise? No one. He had to make it look real.

So real, he even went as far as to wear clothing that matched Greg's, complete with mustache and all, as well as renting the same car model as Greg has. And Drake kept sending Greg pictures of me so he would get pissed off and come to my house. Even told him where I lived.

I'm not sure if I liked that part, but at least it got me the alibi I needed to kill the son of a bitch.

I didn't know Drake had wiretapped me. I had honestly believed it was Greg. But he told me just now he did it. And it can only make me grin.

Another thing he never told me was that he used to be a teacher. Drake was always very quiet about his past, and when he finally came clean to me, I felt so much closer to him.

There's no one in the world I admire more than I admire him.

Together, we concocted a devious plan no one would see coming.

Greg ruined my life, and in exchange, I would ruin his. That was the promise I made to myself the moment I stepped onto that bus and left his house forever. Drake agreed upon that the moment he stepped back into my life.

As he said, he never really left me.

He was always there, watching over me.

The only thing we weren't prepared for was my husband hiring someone to shoot me. Luckily, his plan didn't succeed. But I bet he knew exactly what was coming for him. That's why he thought he needed to get rid of me first. He was right.

When Drake gave me the audio tape, I knew it was time to choose. My parents or my life. I chose me. I gave them a chance, and they didn't take it. I don't regret having Drake murder them. Not even for one second.

They never loved me … and when I realized that, I renounced my love for them.

I closed my heart and let them feel the pain they made me suffer all this time.

I hope they learned their lesson.

And I hope Greg learned his too.

I killed him … with my own hands.

For weeks, I prepared.

Each time he came to my house, I let him in a little further, showing the cracks in our relationship to the whole neighborhood. I needed them to witness the extent of his violence in order to justify my actions.

In order to make it sound believable when I said I killed him out of self-defense.

Because that … is a lie.

I killed the son of a bitch because I wanted to … So damn desperately. It was all I could think about, day and night, until the moment finally arrived.

And as the showerhead wire wrapped around his neck, I whispered into his ear, "You should've signed the divorce papers when you still had a chance. Now, I will take everything you own. Your money. Your house. And even your dignity. You'll be known as nothing more than a disgusting rotting body in the ground."

And then I smiled.

I smiled as I watched the life drain from his body.

Because I realized, there and then, that my plan had succeeded.

We played a dangerous game, and only one of us could win.

That person was me.

EPILOGUE

Accompanying Song: "Technically, Missing" by Trent Reznor & Atticus Ross

DRAKE

A week later

Before she was Mrs. Warren, she was supposed to become Mrs. Bryant.

She was my girl.

My only one.

After she had left, I didn't find love. Not a single time with not a single person other than her.

She was the only one I wanted ... and now, I finally have her back.

Once I picked her up from the cemetery where her parents lie, we never once went back to her home or mine. She didn't want to live there in that house that reeked of his stench one more second. And my cabin? Well, it was a means to an end anyway. I only rented it to be close to her, and now that I finally have her back … I don't need that place anymore.

My old apartment is already rented out to someone else, so we opted to find a different place to live. Somewhere entirely different, in a new-to-us city, a place we can start anew.

It's the perfect way to celebrate the end of a chapter to a story that should be written. The only question is … will it be me who pens it down?

I suppose that question is one I will answer later. But for now, I'm content with having her by my side, wherever I go.

A few days ago, we finally found a small place we can call home. It's a small, rural home with an ample yard and a white picket fence. It's not big, but it's perfect for us. We don't need to live larger than life. We just need to live exactly the way we want to … with all the money we could ever dream of.

Will I work again? Maybe. But for now, it's not even needed. We can live royally off the money we clawed away from Greg. And as for her job? Well, she's still working at the library three times a week, but only because she loves books so much.

And right now, it's time for celebrations …

In the middle of the night, we light a campfire in our backyard and bring out all the things that we used to trick Greg. The clothes that I hate so much. All the notes we never shared with the police but kept secret. The prepaid phone I gave her that she hid in a compartment underneath her bed. All the pictures I took of her that I kept with me. Even my gloves along with several other items.

We throw it into the fire.

I smile at her, she smiles back, and I kiss her on the lips, knowing that finally, she is mine and mine alone. And as my arm is around her shoulders, and I pull her in tight for a hug, we watch the fire eat away our sins.

There's one lesson I learned in this game of cat and mouse.

Never play them with a scorned wife.

THANK YOU
FOR READING!

Thank you so much for reading Dirty Wife Games. I hope you enjoyed the story!

For updates about upcoming books, please visit my website, www.clarissawild.blogspot.com or sign up for my newsletter here: www.bit.ly/clarissanewsletter.

I'd love to talk to you! You can find me on Facebook: www.facebook.com/ClarissaWildAuthor, make sure to click LIKE. You can also join the Fan Club:
www.facebook.com/groups/FanClubClarissaWild and talk with other readers!

Enjoyed this book? You could really help out by leaving a review on Amazon and Goodreads. Thank you!

ALSO BY CLARISSA WILD

Dark Romance
Delirious Series
Killer & Stalker
Mr. X
Twenty-One
Ultimate Sin
VIKTOR
Wicked Bride Games

New Adult Romance
Fierce Series
Blissful Series
Ruin

Erotic Romance
The Billionaire's Bet Series
Enflamed Series
Bad Teacher

Visit Clarissa Wild's website for current titles.
http://clarissawild.blogspot.com

ABOUT THE AUTHOR

Clarissa Wild is a New York Times & USA Today Bestselling author, best known for the dark Romance novel Mr. X. Her novels include the Fierce Series, the Delirious Series, Stalker, Twenty-One (21), Ultimate Sin, Viktor, Bad Teacher, and RUIN. She is also a writer of erotic romance such as the Blissful Series, The Billionaire's Bet series, and the Enflamed Series. She is an avid reader and writer of sexy stories about hot men and feisty women. Her other loves include her furry cat friend and learning about different cultures. In her free time she enjoys watching all sorts of movies, reading tons of books and cooking her favorite meals.

Want to be informed of new releases and special offers? Sign up for Clarissa Wild's newsletter: www.bit.ly/clarissanewsletter

Visit Clarissa Wild on Amazon for current titles. http://bit.ly/clarissbooks

Printed in Great Britain
by Amazon

20899671R00154